W9-DEX-843

THE
RIVER
WITCHES

THE
RIVER
WITCHES

Ben Shecter

Harper & Row, Publishers

New York, Hagerstown, San Francisco, London

Library of Congress Cataloging in Publication Data
Shecter, Ben.
The river witches.

SUMMARY: *A young boy becomes caught in the struggle between good witches and bad witches.*
[1. Witchcraft—Fiction] I. Title.
PZ7.S5382Ri   [Fic]   75–25397
ISBN 0-06-025607-9
ISBN 0-06-025608-7 lib. bdg.

for Rebecca

THE
RIVER
WITCHES

1

"Cultivate the devil and you will harvest in the gardens of hell, where only sin and misery grow!" the minister warned his young congregation.

Andrew pictured himself carrying a watering pail in a garden with two plots, one marked sin, the other misery.

"Let this be your guidebook," continued the minister, holding a prayer book high in the air. "Garden with God, and all things healthy and pure will bloom!"

The minister's shiny red face looked as if it had bloomed on a garden vine. Andrew wondered if, in fact, the minister had been grown from seeds planted in his shoes, and his black frock coat concealed a leafy body.

The last Sunday school meeting before the summer recess was concluded with a hymn. The minister's final words were "Grow with God!"

The sermon had been a long one, and it was warm. Andrew had grown restless. He was relieved when it was over.

Pooter waited patiently outside the church for

Andrew. Dogs weren't allowed inside. He heard the minister's warnings. The minister's loud voice carried out of the church and over the surrounding countryside.

Andrew and his sisters, Meg and Ellen, left the small church together. Pooter greeted them; it was a cheerful reunion.

When they were a distance from the church, the children broke into a run.

> *"No more minister*
> *no more preaching,*
> *no more Sunday school teaching!"*

the children sang as they ran home through the meadow. Seeing some bees, they began to trail them, hoping to find the swarm and the wild honey.

"Slow down or you'll run through summer," cried Pooter, "and it's just beginning." Pooter lagged behind, sniffing at rabbit holes and snapping at grasshoppers. He thought the children were silly to run on such a warm day. Especially Andrew, who raced ahead of his younger sisters.

They shouted, "Wait for us!"

But Andrew pretended not to hear them, and he continued on ahead.

It's all right for them to run, Pooter thought, but I'm tired. They didn't work nearly as hard as I did this morning. All they did was go to Sunday school. Farmer Van Aken had me up early, tending to the cows, sheep, and pigs. Pooter sighed when he thought about the big old sow who always gave him a hard time. "She's such a lazy head," he said.

A rabbit crossed Pooter's path, and he began to chase it. That's something to run for, he told himself.

"Pooter!" Andrew called. "Pooter, come here!"

Just when I'm having fun, Pooter thought. "Sorry, Andrew," he said. "I'm having too much fun." And he continued on his chase. Andrew began to chase the dog. Burrs scratched and held fast to his clothing. With each new burr Andrew shouted louder for Pooter.

Meg and Ellen followed Andrew. "Now they're all after me," said Pooter. He watched the white bushy rabbit tail disappear into a patch of foxglove.

Ellen cried out, "I've been stung by a bee!"

Meg ran to her sister's side, and tore her dress. "Oh, look what I've done!" she cried. "I tore my Sunday dress. God is punishing us for singing that song. I suppose we just have to keep our feelings about Sunday school to ourselves."

"I really like Sunday school," said Ellen, watching her bee sting turn into a big red bump.

"You don't like Sunday school either," said Meg. "Don't lie, or you'll go straight to hell for sure."

Ellen put her hands to her ears. "Andrew, tell her to be quiet," she pleaded. "I won't go to hell, will I?"

"No," said Andrew, "but we will go to the stream and put some mud on that bite and get the sting out."

They ran to the stream and Andrew placed some cool mud on Ellen's hand. "Does it feel better?" he asked.

Ellen looked at the mud caked on her hand and didn't answer.

"Does it feel any better?" Andrew asked again.

"Some," said Ellen.

Meg wiped the tears from her younger sister's face with the hem of her dress. "I'm sorry. You won't go to hell." She placed her arm around Ellen's shoulder. "You're next," she said, looking at Andrew.

"What do you mean, I'm next?" he asked, puzzled.

"Ellen and I have been punished, now it's your turn."

"That's the silliest thing I've ever heard. I'm not going to be punished because I sang some dopey song."

"It is *your* turn," said Ellen.

The girls sat and looked at Andrew, expecting something to happen to him.

Pooter joined them at the stream. He jumped in and cooled himself.

"It's your fault too!" said Meg, looking at Pooter.
Pooter shook himself and looked up at Meg and
then at Andrew. "Why is it my fault?" he asked.

"Mother always says he's got the devil in him,"
said Ellen.

"Come here, Pooter," said Andrew.

Pooter walked slowly to the bank, shaking himself
once again. Andrew reached out and gently stroked
the dog's head. "You're nothing but an old burr
ball," he said.

The children gathered around Pooter and began
to remove the burrs.

"Gently, children, gently," he said, stretching out
on the grass and closing his eyes. Pooter yelped a
few times when the going was difficult.

"That's what you get for chasing rabbits," said
Andrew.

Pooter opened his eyes and looked up. "If you
only knew what fun it is," he said.

"Come on, let's get some honey," said Andrew,
getting to his feet.

"No!" cried Ellen. "I hate bees. They can keep
their old honey; I'll never have any again."

"Me neither!" said Meg. "They're mean."

"Well, that leaves me and Pooter," said Andrew.

"Good," said Pooter. He liked being with Andrew more than anyone else.

Hand in hand, Meg and Ellen walked back to the
farm.

The meadow was glazed still by the afternoon sun. Andrew remained at the stream and said, "It's too hot for trailing bees." He took off his clothes and jumped into the stream. Pooter followed. They splashed at each other and rolled about in the water.

"I know we're not supposed to swim on Sunday, the Lord's day, but doing something you shouldn't makes it more fun. What do you think, Pooter?"

Pooter jumped up. "Everything is fun with you," he said.

Andrew dried himself by lying in the high grass. Pooter rested his head on Andrew's stomach. "You're tickling me," Andrew said, laughing. The dog didn't move his head.

"The summer is a good time," whispered Andrew.

It sure is, thought Pooter.

The sun moved downward, and Andrew knew it was time to return home. He arrived at the farm as Meg and Ellen were setting the dinner table. His mother stirred a big pitcher of cold tea, and when she heard Andrew, she called out, "Where have you been and what kind of mischief have you been getting your sisters into?"

Andrew remained silent. "Andrew, did you hear me?" his mother asked.

"Yes, I heard you," answered Andrew, getting uneasy.

"I would like an explanation!" she demanded.

"We were just trying to get some honey," he answered.

His mother shook her head wearily. "On Sunday you don't go searching for honey wearing your best clothes!"

"I'm sorry," said Andrew.

"You should ask the Lord for His forgiveness," said his mother. "Now clean up and get ready for dinner."

Andrew cleaned up and returned to the kitchen. His father came in smelling of barnyard.

I wonder what we are having for dinner, Pooter thought while he sniffed around the stove. At dinner Farmer Van Aken told them about the new lambs that would be arriving any day.

"I want to be there when they are born," said Andrew.

A silence covered the table. Mrs. Van Aken put down her knife and fork and looked at Andrew. "Son, you'll have to be leaving tomorrow for Aunt Elizabeth's. She needs your help. I received a letter from her," said Mrs. Van Aken, taking it out of her apron pocket. She read the letter to herself, shaking her head every once in a while. "She says here that she is not feeling very well and that her clerk has gone off, and that it is difficult to find a replacement, and unless she does she will have to close the shop." Mrs. Van Aken folded the letter. "Andrew, your father and I talked it over and we thought it would be a fine thing if you helped her out until she regains her good health."

Andrew swallowed hard. He looked at his father, hoping he would say something like "On second thought, we really need Andrew around the farm." But he didn't; he just looked down at his plate.

The children knew that Aunt Elizabeth was really awful.

"I won't go!" cried Andrew. "I hate Auntie Lizard—she's an old witch!"

"Don't speak disrespectfully of your elders," scolded Mrs. Van Aken.

Meg and Ellen giggled, because that was the secret name they had all made up for the old woman their mother called Aunt Elizabeth. They could never understand why their mother called her aunt since she wasn't anyone's aunt at all.

The children thought of her as a bossy lady who owned an apothecary shop on the other side of the river and smelled of root medicine.

Andrew looked at his sisters. They looked back. He knew what they were thinking: This is Andrew's punishment.

But why was his so severe, he thought. Was it because he disliked Sunday school more than they did, or was it because he had gone swimming on a day he shouldn't have, or perhaps both?

Whatever the reason, Andrew thought his punishment was unjust. He thought about the Lord looking down and passing judgment upon him. "I think you're unfair," he whispered, raising his eyes upward.

2

The parade of cows from the barn to the meadow was half hidden by the early-morning mist. Farmer Van Aken led the procession, with Pooter at the rear. Andrew watched from the barnyard fence.

Arrangements had been made with their neighbor, old Mr. Emmerling, to take Andrew to the ferry crossing. Andrew was hoping that old man Emmerling's wagon would break down. And Pooter was hoping that his horse would run away. But their hopes shattered when they heard the old man shout, "Whoa, Franny!"

Mrs. Van Aken appeared on the porch with Meg and Ellen. Farmer Van Aken followed Pooter to the barnyard fence. They watched as Andrew gathered up his belongings and walked toward the wagon.

"Ready, boy?" asked the old man.

Andrew nodded his head yes and climbed aboard the wagon. He sat next to the old man. Pooter ran under the fence and toward the wagon. Franny the horse neighed and pulled her head back, frightened by Pooter's sudden appearance.

Pooter looked up at Andrew. "Don't go," he said.

Andrew bit hard into his lip and said, "Be good, Pooter."

As the wagon moved slowly out of the barnyard, Andrew waved good-bye to his family. Pooter followed the wagon to the big elm tree that marked the entrance to the farm.

The mist disappeared as the sun climbed. Andrew kept looking back until the farm became part of the patchwork landscape. "It's going to be another hot day," said the old man. He didn't speak too much, but when he did it was usually about the weather.

Old Mr. Emmerling smelled like the feed bags he was going to refill at the ferry crossing. The trip there was a long one, and Andrew wondered what the old man and he could talk about.

The wagon moved slowly under dark rows of arched trees and through warm sunny fields. Whenever Andrew tried to start up a conversation, the old man merely nodded. Andrew remained silent and thought about what the family would be doing on the farm at that moment. He wondered if Meg and Ellen were finishing their scarecrow.

At the covered bridge where the stream widened, Mr. Emmerling unhitched Franny and let her cool her feet in the water. Andrew sat on the bank tossing pebbles into the water and wishing Pooter was with him so they could have a good swim together.

Sunlight making its way through cracks and knot-
holes patterned the inside of the covered bridge.
Wooden planks echoed loudly as the wagon wheels
passed over them.

Andrew shouted, "Hello," to hear it returned to
him many times over. The old man looked at him
and smiled.

"Hungry?" asked Mr. Emmerling.

"Yes, sir," said Andrew.

"We'll be nearing Tack Tavern soon," said the
old man. "We can eat there."

Tack Tavern was an old fieldstone house nestled
in a shady pine grove. Hidden birds chattered in the
trees. As the wagon pulled up in front, a dog barked.
Andrew felt his heart skip; he was hoping it was
Pooter who had found his way there. But it wasn't.
A little black-and-white dog ran out of the tavern
and greeted them noisily. When Andrew got down
from the wagon, the dog jumped up into his arms
and gave his face a good washing.

A big friendly-looking man with a red beard and
mustache appeared at the doorway and laughed.

"Sally got herself a new young man," he said.

The little dog rested in Andrew's arms as if they
were a cradle. Her black eyes were fixed on him.

"I know someone you'd really like," said Andrew.

"But I really like you," said Sally Tack.

The tavern keeper and Mr. Emmerling greeted

each other like old friends. Sally wriggled free from
Andrew's arms and joined the two men. She
scratched at old Mr. Emmerling's legs, wanting his
attention.

"Fickle little girl," laughed Andrew.

It was dark and cool inside the tavern. A cider
smell hung in the room. A square-shouldered boy
with strong features who was not much older than
Andrew sat in a corner and ate hurriedly. He looked
up at the group when they entered the tavern. His
eyes were keen and searching.

Sally kept her distance from his table, eyeing him
from some unseen barrier. After they were seated
for a while, the boy left. Mr. Tack sat down with
Andrew and Mr. Emmerling. He looked around the
room before he spoke, and when he did it was in a
hushed voice.

"That was Peter Bronck. He's on an errand to
Uncle Hendrick."

The mention of the name Uncle Hendrick
brought a gasp from old Mr. Emmerling. Andrew
was startled and curious at the old man's reaction.
He looked at the tavern keeper for a further explanation.

Mr. Tack looked at Andrew. "The boy doesn't
know about Uncle Hendrick?" He said it with a
touch of surprise.

Andrew shook his head no. He wondered if

Uncle Hendrick was anything like Auntie Lizard.

The tavern keeper drew himself close to Andrew and his eyes grew large as he spoke. "Uncle Hendrick has the power to fight the witches, and only Peter Bronck, who is a seventh son, is able to serve as a summoner of Uncle Hendrick."

"Who needs Uncle Hendrick?" old Mr. Emmerling asked.

Mr. Tack shrugged. "It's a secret," he said. "But one thing is certain: The bad witches are at work!"

Old Mr. Emmerling nodded his head. "True," he whispered.

"The witches will make it very difficult for the boy to reach his destination, placing many obstacles in his way." The more the tavern keeper spoke, the wider his eyes opened. Andrew was waiting for them to pop out onto the table. He listened attentively, frightened and intrigued by the talk of witches and their power. Mr. Tack excused himself and left the table.

"Have you ever seen a witch?" Andrew asked Mr. Emmerling.

"Witches are very clever at disguising themselves," said Mr. Emmerling. "They conceal their identities from others."

"Can't you tell them by the broomsticks they carry?" asked Andrew.

Mr. Emmerling laughed. "Andrew, my lad, that's an old notion. There is a way of telling, though," he said.

"What is it?" asked Andrew eagerly.

The old man mused for a while. "It's a very dangerous way!"

"Dangerous!" cried Andrew.

"Yes, because you have to get real close to them to know," said old Mr. Emmerling.

"How close?" sighed Andrew.

"Close enough to smell them."

"What kind of smell? Is it like a hog barn?" asked Andrew.

"That, lad, I don't know. My mother, rest her soul, had an encounter with a witch, and she told me that once you smell one you never forget it."

Andrew took a deep breath, trying to remember strange smells, and then he said, "I smell food."

Mr. Tack returned with a tray piled high with bread, cheese, and some early vegetables. He also carried a large pitcher of apple cider. Sally followed the tavern keeper to the table.

The cider was cold and Andrew drank his quickly. Mr. Tack smiled. "It's a thirst-making day," he said, and refilled Andrew's mug.

Sally looked up at Andrew. "How about some cheese?" she asked.

"How would you like some cheese?" said Andrew as he gave a piece to the dog.

"She's a natural-born beggar," said the tavern keeper.

"I'm not a beggar," said Sally. "I just happen to like good food." She pawed at Andrew's arm, wanting more cheese.

"You're just like Pooter," said Andrew.

Pooter? thought Sally. What's a Pooter?

"I'm sure you'd both get along fine," said Andrew, laughing, and he bit into a piece of cheese.

Suddenly the ruff on Sally's neck bristled and her friendly sound turned to a growl. A bent old man appeared at the tavern doorway. There was a charred look about him, as if he had spent most of his life in a chimney. He made his way slowly to the scrap table that was set aside for poor travelers.

"Hush, Sally," said Mr. Tack. "Is that any way to greet a poor wayfarer?"

Sally ran under the table and continued her growling.

Andrew tried to sneak a look at the strange-looking man, but it didn't go unnoticed. The old traveler smiled at him.

Andrew felt uncomfortable, and he was sorry he had done it. He had the awful feeling of being caught.

3

Meg and Ellen put down the bushel of strawberries they were carrying and sat down, resting against the cool well-house wall. Pooter joined them. Meg gave her younger sister a strawberry and took one for herself. "I'm going to miss Andrew," she sighed.

"Me too," said Ellen. "Even though he can be a tease at times."

"I miss him already," said Pooter.

"I hope Andrew doesn't get ill at Auntie Lizard's," said Ellen.

"How could he help getting ill," said Pooter. "Just looking at her face is enough to do it."

"Getting ill at Auntie Lizard's means all those crazy remedies of hers," said Meg, helping herself to another strawberry.

"Remember the time we were all in bed with sore throats and she told us to put a live mouse in a sack and wear it around our necks?" cried Ellen.

"Ugh!" moaned Meg. "I'll never forget that visit. You know, when you think about it, the only time we see Auntie Lizard is when someone is ill, and her cures are worse than the illnesses."

"For sure!" said Pooter, remembering a flea remedy of hers that had made him sneeze for weeks.

"How come Mother always goes along with her and her ideas?" questioned Ellen.

"I've often thought about that," said Meg. "Although I must admit that Mother does act strangely sometimes."

"You can say that again," said Pooter. "I remember when Mother threatened to turn me into a cat. And all I did was taste some stew."

"I wonder where Andrew is now," said Ellen, helping herself to still another strawberry.

"If you don't stop picking on the strawberries, you will get ill, and then you can join Andrew at Auntie Lizard's for one of her bellyache treatments." Meg got up, taking the bushel herself.

"Never," said Ellen, spitting out a half-eaten strawberry.

Outside the tavern, the bright sun seemed to fix things into place. The sounds of the birds had been replaced by the steady hum of the insects. Mr. Emmerling and Andrew climbed onto the wagon and said good-bye to Mr. Tack and Sally.

The roads were dry and Andrew felt his face get a mask of dust on it. He also felt the dust covering his teeth, and he wished for another glass of cider.

Images of being chased by foul-smelling witches

filled Andrew's head, and he found himself looking over his shoulder expecting to see one.

"It's as hot as Hades," murmured the old man.

"It sure is," whispered Andrew, wondering just how hot Hades really was. The more Andrew thought about Hades, the warmer he felt. He tried to push the steamy images out of his head by replacing them with thoughts of paradise. Paradise was surely a cool place, he told himself. With streams and waterfalls, and gentle breezes. He thought of the hillside near the house and the butterflies that sometimes covered it, and then he thought of Pooter chasing them. A loneliness settled upon Andrew.

"I envy you, boy," said Mr. Emmerling. "You'll be getting some relief from the heat, ferrying across the river."

Andrew looked at the old man. "I suppose so," he said gloomily.

Andrew really wanted to say, "Don't envy me, you've never met Auntie Lizard." He also wanted to say, "Don't leave me at the ferry landing—I'll be going back with you." But he didn't.

"Where will you be taking the ferry to?" the old man asked.

"Wiltwyck Landing," answered Andrew.

Mr. Emmerling turned and looked at Andrew. For the second time that day the calm expression the old man wore was shaken away.

"Wiltwyck Landing!" he cried.

"Yes," said Andrew. "That's where Auntie Liz—Elizabeth lives. Have you ever been there?"

"No," answered the old man quickly. "And I don't think I'd care to go there either!"

"Why?" asked Andrew, startled by Mr. Emmerling's response.

"O-o-h—" he stammered, "the people there just ain't my kind of folks."

If the people there were anything like Auntie Lizard, Andrew could understand why.

Mr. Emmerling changed the subject. "I think we're in for a hot summer," he said.

Andrew nodded in agreement, but his thoughts were somewhere else. He closed his eyes, remembering the strong medicine smell that Auntie Lizard carried with her, and how he and his sisters would hold their noses when her back was turned. Pooter refused to be in the same room with her. A dizziness came to Andrew. Pondering the smell, he almost fell from his wagon seat.

It was difficult for Andrew to imagine how he could be of any help to Auntie Lizard, since he knew nothing about working in an apothecary shop. He had never even been in one, and furthermore, he didn't know how to spell the word apothecary.

Thinking more and more about his mission, Andrew grew puzzled. It seemed odd that Auntie Lizard, who prided herself on being an expert on illnesses and their cures, couldn't find a remedy for herself.

A large snake coiled on the road moved swiftly as the wagon approached. Franny the horse heaved and neighed, jolting the wagon. Mr. Emmerling held on to the reins tightly. "Take it easy, girl," he said. "It's only an old snake sunning himself."

Andrew watched as the snake slithered into a row of milkweed. "He sure was big," said Andrew.

"A pet for a witch." The old man chuckled.

The road turned and wove downhill, passing the tannery. Dark potato-shaped clouds made their way out of the tannery smokestacks and drifted, touching other clouds and turning the sky into a field of giant potatoes.

"We're nearing the river," Mr. Emmerling announced.

A scared feeling took hold of Andrew. A fistlike tightness moved into his stomach and settled there, causing a pain. Andrew sighed deeply, hoping to rid himself of the tightness.

"You all right?" Mr. Emmerling asked.

Andrew nodded his head yes, not wanting the old man to know how he really felt.

By the time they reached the ferry crossing, all the potato-shaped clouds had met and joined each other. A great dark cloud hung over the river.

Mr. Emmerling's predictions of a cool river breeze proved to be untrue. The air was weighty and humid; all river activity seemed to be at a stand-still. Andrew got down from the wagon. He thanked Mr. Emmerling and patted Franny the horse on the nose, then bid them a reluctant good-bye.

When the wagon was no longer in view, Andrew walked to the pier, feeling very alone. He was sur-prised when he saw the boy from the tavern waiting there.

A smoky dusk shrouded the other side of the river, pushing it summers away. An uncomfortable silence grew between the two boys. And before it got really unbearable, Andrew said, "It sure is hot!" With an exaggerated gesture he pretended to wipe perspiration off his forehead.

The boy acknowledged the comment by a nod of his head. Andrew turned to the river and whistled nervously. "I wonder where the ferry is," he said.

"So do I," said the boy anxiously.

Andrew was happy that he answered this time with words. Andrew then introduced himself.

The boy hesitated a moment, then he put his hand out. "Nice to know you. I'm Peter Bronck."

While exchanging handshakes, Andrew was seized by the awful thought that perhaps it was a mistake to be friendly with this boy, a target for witches. Andrew wondered if as a result of the handshake he too would become their target.

Oh, what's a handshake? Andrew told himself,

trying to put aside all fears. Anyway, there isn't anyone around.

The sultry evening fell in layers, changing definite shapes into blurs and blots. A charred blot moved toward the pier. Andrew jumped. "Is this the first attack?" he asked himself. And if it was, what would it be like? He knew that witches were capable of anything.

As the gray shape drew closer, Andrew recognized it as the old wayfarer from the tavern. Like a watchful deer, Peter Bronck seemed to position himself for a great leap. He kept this guarded stance until the old traveler spoke.

"Is this the way to the Nieuw Dorp Inn?" he inquired. He spoke with difficulty, as if his voice had been charred also.

"I-I-I've never been this way before," said Andrew. "I'm sorry I can't be of any help, sir."

Peter Bronck said nothing. The old traveler melded into the gauzy darkness. An unwelcome chill enveloped Andrew, and he trembled.

"D-d-o you think he's really lost?" asked Andrew, his teeth chattering.

Peter Bronck answered, his eyes searching the darkness. "If he is, I'm sure he will find his destination."

An icy edge tinged the boy's tone; it cut through the heavy air like a newly sharpened scythe.

Veiled lights flickered in distant waterfront buildings. One small light like a dim fallen star moved along the shore to the pier. "Hallo!" a voice called out.

Andrew stiffened. Still expecting a sudden attack, he was afraid to respond.

"Hallo!" the voice called again.

"Hallo!" answered Peter Bronck in a loud clear voice.

A plump woman appeared with one lighted lantern held high and another unlighted one at her side. She swung the lighted one between the two boys. "Hello, lad," she said, recognizing Peter. "Off on another errand?" she inquired. "What is it this time?" she asked, bending down to light the other lantern.

"You know better than that, Widow Wessels," said Peter, taking on the attitude of an older boy.

"There is no harm in asking, lad. Take no offense. You know that I'm just a lonely old widow hungry for news." The woman grinned. Her teeth were widely spaced, and in the lantern glow her face became a Halloween pumpkin.

Andrew's curiosity was piqued; he too wondered about Peter Bronck's mission. It was obvious to Andrew from the woman's familiarity with Peter Bronck that he must have made this trip many times before to summon Uncle Hendrick.

A feeling of admiration for Peter Bronck grew within Andrew. He was a brave and selfless boy who acted as a courier for those in need.

"Ferry is late," announced the plump widow, walking with a waddle toward the end of the pier. "Must be some kind of trouble."

"Trouble?" asked Andrew.

"Happens from time to time," the woman answered wearily. She placed one lantern at the pier's edge. "There!" she said matter-of-factly. "If and when the ferry arrives, it'll dock safely. I've done my job," she said, leaving the pier.

"Good night, Widow Wessels," Peter Bronck called out after her.

"Good night, lads," she called back. "And good luck!" Her voice sounded far away.

The boys watched her light until it became a fallen star again.

A silence welled between the two boys, and this time Peter Bronck took it upon himself to break it. "Where are you headed?" he asked.

"Auntie Li—" Andrew caught himself. "I'm going to visit an aunt at Wiltwyck Landing." Andrew thought a moment. "She really isn't an aunt, just a friend of my mother's, but we've always called her auntie. Her real name is Miss Elizabeth Hardwell."

"The apothecary shop proprietress?" asked Peter Bronck.

"That's the one," answered Andrew, surprised that he knew of her. "Do you know her?"

"I don't know her personally, but I know some-one who does." Peter Bronck looked at Andrew suspiciously.

"Have you ever seen her?" asked Andrew.

"On one or two occasions," answered Peter.

"Then you know what she looks like. If you prom-ise not to tell anyone, I'll tell you the secret name my sisters and I have for her."

"I promise," said Peter.

"We call her Auntie Lizard."

"That's a good name for her," said Peter Bronck, laughing, "because she sure looks like one."

Peter's laugh was a good sound, and it made An-drew feel happy.

The boys sat side by side at the end of the pier watching insects gather around the lantern light. Fish made reflections quiver, and one large moth became a dinner for them.

The clattering sound of horses and a wagon echoed through the night. As the sound grew louder, a familiar frightened feeling returned to An-drew, his heart raced, and his body trembled. This is it for certain, he told himself.

The boys strained their ears as they heard muffled voices. "If only the ferry would come," whispered Andrew.

Peter Bronck got to his feet. The sound of the

wagon faded, and the planks on the pier told of someone approaching.

A tall man burdened with packages materialized in the dim light.

"Did I miss the ferry?" he asked.

"It didn't even get here yet," Andrew responded quickly.

"Oh, good," said the man, collapsing under his packages.

Paintbrushes protruded from beneath his hatband like quills on a porcupine's back. He removed his hat and placed it carefully alongside himself, and then he smoothed his shiny dark hair with a long silk neckerchief.

His appearance was that of a dismembered grasshopper, and Andrew couldn't help but see this. He held back a giggle and pretended to cough. He didn't want to offend the stranger.

"What beastly weather," the stranger sighed. "I feel as if I'm being buried." He searched wearily through his packages and removed a cardboard that had been carelessly tucked away. Its ends were frayed, and daubs of paint marked one side. He began to fan himself with it. At first the fanning was vigorous, but it was soon replaced by a slower, lazier rhythm. The man had his eyes closed and he wore an expression of delicious indulgence.

After a while he put his fan aside and opened his

eyes. He looked at Andrew. "How rude of me!" he said. "Allow me to introduce myself. I am Ashton Dansforth, the portraitist. Perhaps you've heard of me?"

Andrew shook his head no, feeling dumb and almost ashamed that he didn't recognize the name. At the same time it also made Andrew unwilling to relinquish his own name.

Ashton Dansforth focused his attention on Peter. "I didn't even see you!" he cried. "It's a black night."

"That it is!" said Peter, stepping into the shadows. "That it is!"

A strange, dank, cellarlike odor vaporized in their midst. Lingering, its presence became an intrusion like an uninvited guest.

Peter stepped deeper into the shadows. And Andrew fought desperately with his senses to recall and associate the smell.

5

"Dinner just wasn't the same without Andrew," said Ellen.

"You can say that again!" said Pooter, who missed the extra scraps that Andrew would hand him under the table.

"Now, now, girls, don't get yourselves unhappy. Your brother will be home before you know it," said Mrs. Van Aken.

"Before you know it can be a long time," said Pooter.

The girls set the oil lamp on the table and took their samplers from the small blanket chest their father had built for them. Andrew had painted it blue.

"I'm going to give my sampler to Andrew," said Ellen. "I think I'll embroider his name on it."

"What a nice idea," said Mrs. Van Aken.

"And I'm going to embroider Pooter's face on mine and give it to Andrew for his birthday," said Ellen.

"Now that should be a good-looking sampler," said Pooter.

Farmer Van Aken took his pipe from the pipe box that hung alongside the fireplace and went outside. Pooter followed him.

The farmer tapped his unlit pipe against the porch railing, and removed a worn tobacco pouch from his pocket. He stuffed his corn pipe and lit it, and then he took a deep puff.

"I wish Farmer Van Aken would let me have a puff on his pipe," said Pooter. "It must be good—he sure seems to enjoy it."

Farmer Van Aken watched the smoke disappear into the dark, starless night. "We've been shut off from the heavens," he said.

"It certainly is a dark night," said Pooter, rubbing himself against Farmer Van Aken's leg trying to roust some fleas.

"I wonder where Andrew is right now," said the farmer, looking at Pooter.

"Wherever he is, I wish I were with him," said Pooter. "He's the best friend I've got."

"I know you two are good friends; I'm sure he's going to miss you," said the farmer.

The kitchen door opened and Mrs. Van Aken came onto the porch carrying the butter churn. "Talking to yourself?" she inquired.

"No, I was talking to Pooter," said Farmer Van Aken.

"What did he have to say?" she said, smiling.

"Nothing you'd be interested in," said Pooter.

"If you must know, we were talking about Andrew and how we miss him, and how it's your fault that Andrew went away, you and your Auntie Lizard!"

Mrs. Van Aken looked down at Pooter. "Now why is that dog snapping so viciously? I get the distinct impression that Pooter is angry with me."

"Don't be silly, dear," said Farmer Van Aken, drawing a deep puff on his pipe. "We were talking about Andrew."

"Oh?" said Mrs. Van Aken. She began to turn the long wooden ladle inside the crock. "What about Andrew?"

"It is his first time away from home. I hope he'll be all right," said the farmer. "Did you pack his prayer book?"

"I think so," said Mrs. Van Aken reflectively. "I'm sure I did."

"Then there's nothing to worry about," said the farmer, contentedly watching the smoke curl from his pipe.

When the churning was done, Farmer Van Aken helped his wife into the house. Pooter went up to the loft. Andrew's bed looked very empty. Pooter climbed on top of it and closed his eyes, pretending that Andrew was there and that he would get a good rubbing any minute. The rubbing never happened and Pooter opened his eyes.

As he grew accustomed to the darkness, Pooter was able to see the wall pegs for Andrew's clothing, the blanket chest at the foot of the bed, and the small leather-bound prayer book on top of it.

"The prayer book!" said Pooter. "Mrs. Van Aken forgot to pack it." Pooter was surprised by his discovery, because he knew Mrs. Van Aken to be a very thorough person.

It was stiflingly warm in the loft, and Pooter found sleeping difficult. He was also troubled about Andrew. He grew restless and left the house through an open window, taking the prayer book with him.

By the time Pooter reached the knoll behind the house he had made the decision.

I'm going to join Andrew at Auntie Lizard's, he told himself. Anyway, Andrew needs his prayer book, and I'm the one to deliver it!

Pooter left the Van Aken farm hoping the rest of the family would understand. "If I could only write a note," he said. Pooter went off into the night with only his senses to guide him.

Peter Bronck was lost in the deep fold of a shadow. He remained silent and had suddenly become an invisible night creature.

"Be careful, lad. Don't fall into the water!" said Ashton Dansforth. "It would be difficult to fish you out on a night such as this."

Andrew wished that Peter Bronck would stop being so mysterious and step back into the light again. He felt uncomfortable being alone with the painter, just the two of them sharing the light. There was something decidedly peculiar about him, something that Andrew didn't like. He wasn't sure what it was, but he felt a discomfort, and that was enough to keep him at his distance.

A feeble light moved on the river. "It's the ferry!" shouted Andrew, happy to see the light. "I think it's the ferry, I hope it's the ferry," he murmured, crossing all his fingers.

"It is the ferry!" said Peter, reappearing in the lantern light.

"Good!" said Ashton Dansforth. "I'm exhausted." He stood up, stretching. "Excuse me," he

said, covering a yawn. "Visiting family?" he asked Andrew.

"No!" said Andrew. "She's no family of mine!"

"Who is she?" asked the painter.

"Oh, no one you would know," answered Andrew, quickly and quietly.

"Try me," he said. "I know lots of people, and know a lot about people," he bragged.

Peter Bronck stood at the end of the pier swinging the lantern back and forth, guiding the ferry to port.

Unexplainably, the lantern light was extinguished, and the darkness clamped down like hands over one's eyes.

"What happened?" shouted Andrew.

"I don't know!" answered Peter. His voice rang with urgency. "We need light!"

"Mr. Dansforth, have you a match?" asked Andrew, feeling uneasy near him in the darkness.

"No," he answered.

"I have an idea," said Peter. "Let us shout. The ferry will come toward our sound."

Peter and Andrew started shouting. "Mr. Dansforth, why aren't you shouting?" asked Andrew.

"It's too hot to shout," came the reply.

Angered, Peter said, "I'm sure you'll find that you won't be too hot to get on the ferry when it docks."

"If it docks," said Ashton Dansforth.

"It will dock all right, in spite of you," said Peter.

"You boys will have to do the shouting for me. Try to understand, I'm a very poor shouter."

"Try!" said Andrew. "Please try!" he pleaded.

"Save your breath, Andrew. I've met his type before," said Peter.

"You have?" said Andrew, frightened. He knew what Peter was implying.

Just as the ferry was only shouts away, its lights were extinguished also.

"Oh no!" cried Andrew.

"Oh yes!" said the painter. His voice had a hollow sound to it.

Just then a bolt of heat lightning split through the blackness with an incandescence that illuminated the river and shore for miles around. The lightning came in rapid succession.

The boat neared the dock and the ferryman waved his arms joyfully.

Andrew and Peter waved back.

"See, you did quite well without me," said Ashton Dansforth, looking like a road-show magician in the eerie silver-blue light.

The ferryman tossed a rope to Peter. He missed it at first, but caught the second throw. And he held the rope tightly.

"Peter, is that you?" the ferryman called out.

"Yes, Mr. Gaty, it's me!" answered Peter.

Andrew felt a temporary sense of relief; it seemed another ally had joined them.

"A black night," said the ferryman. "Strange things have been occurring."

"I might have known," whispered Peter.

"I was stuck on a mud bank—thought I'd never get free of it. Young Timothy Sills came by with his sloop and gave me a tug. And when the lights were extinguished I thought for sure I'd never get here, but this lightning was surely a miracle," Mr. Gaty said, out of breath.

"Do you believe in miracles?" asked Ashton Dansforth, gathering his belongings and preparing to set foot on the ferry.

"If this lightning isn't a miracle, then I don't know what is," said the ferryman.

Andrew thought miracles happened only in the Bible, and that they stopped when the Bible ended.

"Don't let him set foot on this ferry, Mr. Gaty," said Peter.

"Why not?" The ferryman looked at Peter, surprised.

"He's a bearer of ill tidings, to put it mildly," said Peter.

"What's he talking about?" the ferryman questioned Ashford Dansforth.

"If you must know, sir, it has to do with my shouting. I didn't want to shout, I'm just not a shouter. Now if you'll excuse me, I would appreciate passage to the other side of the river. And as you can see I haven't a ferry of my own; therefore, a trip of yours is most necessary."

"Have you the fare?" asked Mr. Gaty.

"Do I look like a pauper?"

"Looks are deceiving!" Andrew spoke up.

"I beg your pardon!" said Ashton Dansforth, his eyes narrowing to slits. "This is all very silly. Please, sir, my trip across is really quite urgent."

"He's lying," cried Andrew, who was not put off by the painter's menacing expression. "A little while ago he acted as if he didn't care if the ferry got here or not."

"Is that true?" asked the ferryman.

"As I explained to you before, it all has to do with shouting. I should say, not shouting. You see, as a child my mother told me never to shout, and now I find it a difficult task. I'm sure a man of your worldy travels would understand a thing like that."

The steady lightning was joined by the sound of thunder—a rumbling so loud that it seemed to shake the pier from its moorings.

"A storm is brewing for sure," said Mr. Gaty, securing the ferry. "I'm afraid we all won't be going anywhere!"

"Something is definitely brewing!" said Peter Bronck.

The wind pulled across Pooter's path, trees swayed and bent, leaves and twigs twirled in a night dance. Pooter held fast to the prayer book. When the first drops of rain touched his nose, Pooter decided to seek shelter. "For the safety of the book," he told himself. He hunted around for a good cover, and by the time the rainfall had grown heavy, he had found a moss-carpeted hollow alongside a fallen oak. "A good place," he said, curling up while waiting for the rain to pass.

The river lapped angrily at the shores, making seemingly immovable objects water bound.

Mr. Gaty had difficulty securing his ferry, and he asked Peter Bronck for a helping hand. On board, the ferryman and Peter worked feverishly to keep the ferry docked.

Just when they thought they had succeeded, the tie line broke and the ferry moved away from the pier. Not wanting to be left alone with Ashton Dansforth, Andrew took a running jump and leaped onto the ferry. He missed a watery ordeal in the surging river by a fraction of an inch.

"Whew!" cried Peter. "Good jump!" He put his arm around Andrew.

Ashton Dansforth ran to the end of the pier shouting, "Wait for me! Wait for me!"

"He's shouting!" cried Andrew. "Listen, he's shouting!"

The ferryman mumbled angrily to himself, "And I almost believed his story about his mother telling him not to shout."

The ferry spun as if caught in a great churn. At times Andrew felt as if the boat were being pulled upward. He wondered if, when the wind and rain stopped, like Noah's Ark the ferry would be planted high on a mountain.

Mr. Gaty, Peter, and Andrew huddled under a tarpaulin. The rain hit the canvas, reminding Andrew of the shower of hickory nuts that fell on the barn roof in autumn. He took comfort in the familiar sound.

Andrew couldn't help but take some delight in the adventure he was now experiencing. Danger seemed a faraway thing. He felt secure nestled between Peter Bronck and Mr. Gaty. It was a cozy feeling, like being under a blanket with good friends.

Mr. Gaty told river stories, and Andrew thought

it would be a good thing to be a ferryman when he grew up. Then Mr. Gaty sang a river chantey, and Peter and Andrew joined him.

Hear the wind blow, boy,
hear the wind blow.
Hold on to your sails, boy,
or get set for a row.

When their singing ended, Peter took notice of the quiet. "It's stopped raining!" he shouted.

"And we've stopped tossing!" cried Andrew.

Mr. Gaty stood up and threw the tarpaulin aside. "It's going to be a fine day!" he cheerfully announced.

The river mirrored the amber glow of a new summer day. Mr. Gaty steered the ferry toward Wiltwyck Landing. Suddenly Andrew thought about Auntie Lizard, and if she was as sick as she claimed to be. He wondered if she would still be alive when he reached her.

"Ugh!" said Pooter, shaking himself off. "I feel like a damp mop that worked over a floor of wet leaves." He stretched, yawned, and rubbed his back against the bough of the fallen tree. "I'm hungry," said Pooter. He listened to his stomach grumble. He sniffed around hoping to discover something good to eat, but all he uncovered was a fat grumpy toad who preferred not to be eaten.

Pooter took up the prayer book and continued on his journey. He headed for the road and hoped to pick up Andrew's trail, but the heavy rain had washed away any chance of that happening. Dwarfed by a long row of towering elms, Pooter felt very alone, and lost. He continued at a brisk pace, hoping he could somewhere pick up a familiar scent.

Pond-sized puddles extended over and beyond the road, creating muddy detours. "A good road for the sow," he said. Then Pooter thought about the barnyard and wondered how Farmer Van Aken would be getting along without him. "I'm sure he'll manage," said Pooter. "But not as well."

An early-morning haze shielded Tack Tavern, and if not for little Sally's barking, Pooter might not have noticed it.

"A friendly voice," said Pooter upon hearing Sally. He made his way to the tavern.

Sally was the only one who was up and about at Tack Tavern. She was surprised and a little frightened when Pooter made his appearance. He was caked with mud. Pooter sensed Sally's fright and he approached cautiously.

"Don't be afraid," he said when he got close enough to speak in his normal voice.

Sally was silent for a moment before she spoke. "I

must confess, you had me startled and confused. At first I didn't know what you were."

"Why?" asked Pooter puzzled.

"Well, you are strange-looking," she said.

"Strange-looking?" cried Pooter.

"You've got a coat of mud on you that would make any hog absolutely rage with envy," said Sally.

Pooter suddenly felt embarrassed. "I'm not usually this way," he explained uncomfortably. "The road is muddy. You see, I've been traveling; I just have to get this book to a friend of mine."

"I was wondering what you were carrying," she said.

"It's a prayer book," said Pooter. "And Andrew left home without it."

"Who is Andrew?" asked Sally.

"He's my friend," said Pooter proudly. "And I'm Pooter."

"Pooter!" cried Sally.

Pooter had a terrible itch and he tried to ignore it rather than scratch it in front of Sally. He felt as if he had already made a bad impression. So he squirmed and turned, but the itch grew worse. Unable to stand it any longer, Pooter gave himself a good scratching as well as a few rolls on the ground. Relieved, he got to his feet and apologized for his behavior.

"Pooter, Pooter, Pooter." Sally repeated the

name to herself. "Where have I heard that name before?"

"You've heard of me?" asked Pooter, wide-eyed with surprise.

"Yes, I did hear of you from a very nice-looking boy, unless there is another Pooter," said Sally.

"There's only one Pooter, and that's me," said Pooter boastfully. "And the nice-looking boy is my friend Andrew."

Pooter was pleased that Andrew had mentioned his name.

"What did Andrew say about me?" he asked.

"Something about your appetite," said Sally.

"Oh, did you have to remind me?" said Pooter, his stomach grumbling loudly. "I'm starved."

"Poor dear Pooter," said Sally sympathetically. "I know the feeling. Perhaps I can help you out."

"You can?" asked Pooter, jumping joyfully.

"I'll try," said Sally. "Just wait here."

"I promise I won't go anyplace," he said.

Pooter lay down and rested his head on the prayer book. "I don't know your name," he called out.

"Sally," she said. "My friends call me Sally." She disappeared into the tavern through the lower part of a Dutch door.

Pooter waited, thinking of wonderful things to eat. The wait became a long one, and several times he thought Sally would never return.

When she did, Pooter could see at once that it had

been worth the wait. Sally had some large soup bones.

"For you," she said, giving them to him.

"Thank you, sweet Sally," said Pooter, getting to work on the bones.

After grinding them to a pulp, Pooter looked up and said, "I was sure hungry!"

"Obviously!" said Sally, looking at the meager traces of what once had been two extra-large soup bones.

"Now I'll have the strength to go on," said Pooter. "Do you happen to know in which direction Andrew was traveling?"

"I think I overheard them talking about going toward the river," said Sally.

"Then that's the direction I'd better head in," said Pooter. "I hate to be so impolite as to eat and depart quickly," he said, "but I've got a feeling that Andrew needs me."

"I understand." Sally pointed out the direction. "Have a safe trip," she said. "I hope you find your way to Andrew."

"So do I," said Pooter.

"Come again!" Sally called out.

Pooter headed toward the river.

Flat-bottomed sloops moved easily along the river, dipping slightly as friends do when passing with a nod of recognition. Mr. Gaty steered the ferry to port, cutting through small islands of floating branches, a reminder of the night's storm. "We're here, lads!" he announced.

An anxious pang crossed through Andrew as the ferry bumped against the rocky shore of Wiltwyck Landing. It was difficult for Andrew to imagine what might be in store for him at Auntie Lizard's—all images in his mind were blurred, as if seen through teary eyes.

The boys thanked Mr. Gaty and jumped ashore. Andrew landed on wobbly legs. He didn't know if it was caused by the time spent on the ferry, hunger, or the uncertainty of the immediate future. Perhaps all three. Nevertheless, standing on the ground provided Andrew with a strange physical sensation, one that occurs before toppling over.

"Here's where we part," said Peter Bronck, extending his hand toward Andrew.

Andrew clasped Peter's hand. The grip was

strong. In that handshake Andrew felt a strength that renewed a stronger feeling within himself.

The handshake could not diminish the sadness that Andrew experienced at that moment of parting. He had grown to like Peter Bronck, and wished he could stay on as a friend.

"Where are you headed?" Andrew asked.

Peter pointed to a white church perched on top of a high hill. "That's my destination," he said.

The church resembled a miniature Greek temple. Voluminous white clouds tumbled behind it, and Andrew thought it must be the very gateway to heaven.

Andrew had so convinced himself of this that he asked Peter if he would be returning from there.

At first Peter was puzzled by the nature of the question, and then he smiled and said, "Yes, yes of course I shall be returning. I'm just on an errand."

"Andrew! Andrew Van Aken!" a familiar voice called out.

When Andrew turned and saw who it was, he was once again seized by a strange sensation, and he thought this time he would fall down for certain.

It was Auntie Lizard running toward him with her arms flapping at her sides like broken wings. She appeared to be an ancient flying reptile.

Andrew's mouth dropped open in disbelief. Auntie Lizard was supposed to be very ill, and here she was greeting him, looking very fit.

"Andrew Van Aken, you had me worried to death," exclaimed Auntie Lizard. "I was up all night waiting for you, and I must confess that only the worst thoughts entered my mind." She clutched Andrew to her bosom, and a strange-smelling vapor seemed to be released in that squeeze.

The smell made Andrew sneeze. "Getting a cold, child? Summer colds are the worst kind," she said. "Let's get to the shop immediately. I have just the remedy for you!"

"Oh no!" Andrew moaned to himself. "And I just got here." How could he tell her that it was her smell that made him sneeze, and not a cold?

Auntie Lizard's sudden and unexpected appearance distracted Andrew from Peter Bronck, and when he looked over his shoulder he saw that it was too late. Peter was nowhere in sight.

An emptiness surrounded Andrew. He followed Auntie Lizard in silence, and after a while he said, "I was led to believe that you were ill."

"Ill, what gave you— Oh yes, I was very ill!" she said.

"Then I take it that you are fully recovered," said Andrew.

"Not only am I fully recovered, but, my dear boy, I've never felt better."

The words fell upon Andrew's ears like the sounds of bolts opening. "Then you won't be needing me?" said Andrew excitedly.

Auntie Lizard grew as rigid as a gravestone figure. "Of course I need you! Although my recovery was truly miraculous—" Breaking off in midsentence, she whispered, "I don't often use that word. Anyway, dear Andrew, there is always the threat of a relapse hovering about, and you wouldn't want anything to happen to your old auntie, would you?"

Andrew shook his head in the negative, all the while really thinking something to the contrary.

They continued on their way, and Auntie Lizard spoke aloud, directing her remark to no one in particular. "This is my busy season, and I need an apprentice!"

Andrew followed behind, dutifully but reluctantly.

Wiltwyck Landing was a small village built on a hill that sloped down to the river. Houses were clustered together, hugging each other as if to prevent themselves from slipping into the river. Twisted chimneys grew from moss-patched roofs as weeds do in a forgotten hillside garden. Viewed from a distance, Wiltwyck Landing gave the impression of being one big rambling house.

The road through the center of the village was not much wider than a footpath. It twisted serpentlike, with a shop at each turn. Overhanging signs reached out, touching, giving the road a ceiling. In places the road narrowed so that when passing, one was obliged to step aside for those carrying baskets or bundles. More than once Andrew found himself pressed up against a building in order to let some-one pass. At one point a basket full of chickens brushed against the tip of his nose.

The sound of the clucking chickens evoked thoughts of home. Andrew wanted to turn and run.

Meg and Ellen ran into the house muddied and sobbing. "We've looked everywhere," they cried. "There isn't a trace of him."

"Where could Pooter possibly have gone to?" asked Mrs. Van Aken.

"Maybe the storm swallowed him up," said Meg.

"Don't say that!" cried Ellen.

"I'm sure he's around somewhere," said Farmer Van Aken, trying to calm his family and hide his own concern. "You know Pooter—he'll show up."

"Probably dead," whispered Meg.

"I heard that," snapped Ellen. "He isn't dead, is he?" Ellen looked at her parents pleadingly.

"No, Pooter isn't dead," said Mrs. Van Aken, stroking her daughter's hair.

Farmer Van Aken bit down hard on the end of his pipe. "There is the possibility that he went after Andrew," he said.

"He wouldn't leave us for Andrew," said Meg. "He knows how much we all love him."

"True," said the farmer. "But Pooter knows that

we all have each other, and right now Andrew has no one."

Mrs. Van Aken spoke up. "Why dear, Andrew has Aunt Elizabeth."

"That's practically the same as having no one," murmured Ellen.

"We'll just have to have faith, and pray that Pooter returns to us," said Farmer Van Aken.

Meg and Ellen had never prayed in the afternoon. It was something they always did before going to bed. Today was different, and Meg told Ellen that they had to pray right away.

"It's an emergency!" she said. "We can't wait until nightfall."

The girls went upstairs and knelt by their beds. "I feel silly," said Ellen, "praying and not going to sleep."

Meg took her younger sister's hand and led her outside. "Let's go to some high place," she said.

They walked to the top of the hill in back of the house and prayed for Pooter's safe return.

"And let's not forget Andrew," said Ellen.

The sisters bowed their heads and cried.

"So this is the river!" said Pooter. "It sure is bigger than the pond." He ran onto the ferry landing.

"What have we here?" said Ashton Dansforth, soggy and rumpled. He eyed Pooter's arrival with some curiosity. Pooter held the prayer book firmly in his mouth.

"A dog that reads," he quipped. "And what may you be reading, pray tell?"

As Pooter neared him, Ashton Dansforth reached down to take the book from his mouth. Pooter snarled and the prayer book dropped.

When Ashton Dansforth saw the title of the book, his fingers became quivering centipedes. "Help! Help!" he shrieked.

"Boy, did I scare him!" said Pooter.

Ashton Dansforth sat at the edge of the pier, clutching his belongings and telling Pooter to keep his distance.

Pooter knew he was a tough-looking and -sounding dog, but no one had ever reacted to him quite that way before, and the tall thin stranger's behavior confounded him.

Mr. Gaty and his small raftlike ferry returned. And when the ferryman saw Ashton Dansforth sitting and waiting, he said with a look of great surprise, "Are you still here?"

"Of course I'm still here," said Ashton Dansforth. A mixture of anger and weariness colored his tone. "How else am I to get to the other side of the river? I don't fly like a bird, and I don't swim like a fish, although I must admit there are some things I do excel in."

"Those boys didn't have much trust in you," said Mr. Gaty.

Pooter's ears perked up. "Did he say boys? I wonder if one of them was Andrew."

"My dear man, I can assure you I am a well-intentioned individual, and I am just eager to get across the river and visit an old friend of mine. Perhaps you know her—she owns an apothecary shop."

"You know Miss Elizabeth Hardwell?" asked Mr. Gaty.

"Quite well," answered Ashton Dansforth exhaustedly.

"He would know Auntie Lizard," said Pooter. "Birds of a feather—"

With a certain degree of hesitation the ferryman said, "Oh—all right, hop aboard."

Ashton Dansforth boarded the ferry with great ceremony. He carefully secured his packages, and then went through some ritualistic procedure of grooming. His fingers became a comb for his long dark hair. He brushed at his clothing vigorously, hoping to remove the spots and wrinkles. It was a futile task.

Pooter thought Ashton Dansforth looked exactly as he had before the cleaning exercise, and he couldn't understand why the strange-looking man went to all the trouble.

At least when I scratch myself, I get rid of a flea or two, Pooter told himself.

"Whose dog is that?" asked the ferryman, pointing to Pooter.

"I'm the Van Akens' dog," said Pooter proudly.

"Just some mongrel looking for a handout," said the painter.

"Don't you call me a mongrel, you rumpled mess of a human being!" Pooter snarled angrily. "Furthermore, for your information I happen to be of very good breeding. My mother always told me my father was a great hunting dog. That's something you can't claim."

Pooter was very touchy when the subject of his background was discussed.

"Let's get going before this heinous animal attacks!" said Ashton Dansforth, hiding behind Mr. Gaty.

"Heinous? I'm part retriever," said Pooter.

The ferry moved away, and Pooter remained on the dock. "I've just got to get to Andrew," he said, and he jumped aboard the ferry.

"Push him off! Push him off!" cried Ashton Dansforth.

"I can't do a thing like that," said Mr. Gaty, looking down at Pooter. "Especially to a dog that carries a prayer book."

The gentle rocking of the boat and the warmth of the early-day sun made Pooter drowsy. He fell asleep using the folded tarpaulin as a bed. Ashton Dansforth sat in a far corner of the ferry, keeping a watchful eye on him.

Seeing Ashton Dansforth all rumpled and disgruntled, Mr. Gaty, a man of compassion, felt some responsibility for his present appearance and state of being. To make amends, he tried to engage the painter in conversation. "Quite a storm last night— unexpected, too!" he said.

"Did you have to remind me?" Ashton Dansforth answered surlily.

"It was like the work of the devil himself," said the ferryman.

"Probably was," the painter said under his breath.

"What was that you said?" asked Mr. Gaty.

"I said it was terrible." Ashton Dansforth heaved a deep sigh.

Mr. Gaty was able to tell by his passenger's response that he wasn't too eager to discuss the storm, and realized that it was an ill-chosen topic for discussion.

Changing the subject, Mr. Gaty said, "Never saw a dog carrying a prayer book before. Do you suppose he can read?" The ferryman tried to joke, but he could tell from the expression on Ashton Dansforth's face that he was in no mood for joking or conversation.

Mr. Gaty steered the ferry in silence, and after a while broke the stillness by whistling.

When Wiltwyck Landing took on the shape of a sprawling house, Ashton Dansforth got to his feet and gathered his things together as if readying himself for some great escape.

The ferry bumped into port, and without so much as a good-bye, the painter leaped ashore like an awkward goose over a stone wall.

Awakened from his deep sleep, Pooter looked around, and when he saw that Ashton Dansforth was no longer there, he too jumped ashore, hoping to find him and the way to Andrew. In his eagerness to pick up the trail of the painter, Pooter left the prayer book behind.

"Hello!" called Peter Bronck, running to the dock with a round old man following him like a rolling ball. It was Uncle Hendrick, the minister. His shirttails were askew, and his shoes were untied.

It was easy to see that he was a man who dressed in haste.

Mr. Gaty greeted him, and both he and Peter helped the old minister aboard the ferry.

"The very devil is at work this time," the old man huffed.

"For sure!" said Peter nodding his head.

"Begging your pardon, may I inquire as to the nature of his doings?" asked the ferryman, eager to hear a story of the devil's mischief.

"If all goes well, I will recount the adventure when we return," said Uncle Hendrick, tucking in his shirttails. Peter, who was carrying his jacket, helped him on with it.

After his clothing was properly arranged, Uncle Hendrick sat down and wiped the perspiration that glistened on his forehead. He raised his white eyebrows. "Those witches are always conjuring up something. They'll be the death of me yet." He sighed.

Peter noticed the prayer book on the ferry. He took the book up and said, "Have you taken to reading this?"

"No," answered Mr. Gaty. "Not that I'm averse to it, but the strangest thing is that it was left behind by a dog."

"Surely you must be jesting," said Uncle Hendrick.

"No, I'm telling the truth—he was carrying it in his mouth."

Peter opened the book and read the inscription on the inside cover aloud. "This prayer book is the property of Andrew Van Aken."

Peter Bronck looked at the prayer book quizzically. "That's the boy who was going to visit Elizabeth Hardwell."

Uncle Hendrick drew his brows down, and he chewed on his bottom lip, giving the impression of someone trying to swallow something totally indigestible. He remained in that pose for a while and then spoke. "What would he be doing with Elizabeth Hardwell? She's never had a book like that in her shop!"

"True," whispered Mr. Gaty.

"I'll bring this book to Andrew when we return," said Peter.

"I'd like to be there when you do," said Uncle Hendrick, "just to see that old crone's expression."

10

Jonas, Auntie Lizard's fat old tabby cat, watched from atop a cupboard as Andrew unpacked his belongings. For his stay there, Andrew was to live in a room above the apothecary shop. It was a small room with a sloped ceiling that reached down and touched a tiny window that was curtained with dust and webs. Irregular wooden beams ran the length of the slope, and fragments of bark clung to them. Pieces that had fallen away carpeted the wide-planked floor.

Like a soldier on guard, the cat was unfaltering in his watch. Andrew felt uneasy confined to the small space with the large cat poised in a pouncing position.

"I'm no bird or mouse," said Andrew, "so if you have any ideas about jumping on me, forget them. As you can plainly see, I'm larger than you are, and stronger too!" Andrew rolled up his shirt sleeve, clenched his fist, and bent his arm, showing a muscle.

A surreptitious smile appeared on the cat's round face. Andrew noticed the change of expression. "If

you are laughing at me," said Andrew somewhat
nervously, "be advised now that you are dealing
with Andrew Van Aken. And let me tell you, I've
handled a mean sow or two back home, and they're
much bigger than you."

A small bell tinkled in the shop below, indicating
that someone had come in. Andrew listened. He
heard voices, the unmistakable sound of two people
in a joyful reunion. Cackling laughter rose from
below and came through the floorboards.

Andrew wondered who it was, and how anyone
could possibly make Auntie Lizard so happy.

Unable to find Ashton Dansforth, and remembering the prayer book he had left behind, Pooter ran
back to the pier. It was too late. The ferry was gone.
"I'm really messing things up!" moaned Pooter.
Frustrated, he barked at the river. His sound echoed
back; it was an empty noise. Pooter sat down unhappily at the river's edge. He was soon joined by the
village rat catcher. The rat catcher carried a cage full
of squealing rats that he dropped into the river,
drowning them.

Pooter didn't wait around for when it was time to
pull up the cage. He returned to the village. There
he roamed around, sniffing everywhere and at
everything, hoping to find Andrew.

He went to the bootmaker, who was fashioning

a high shoe on a wooden form. He watched awhile as the shoe took shape. And he told himself he was happy he didn't have to wear it. His next stop was the carpentry shop, where the carpenter was building a small coffin. "For some poor child," said Pooter sadly. Then he went to the confectionery, where wonderful aromas wafted out into the village.

Its windows were filled with pastries, cakes, pies, tarts, and candies of all shapes, colors, and sizes. "Oh, what a good place!" said Pooter, drooling at the enchanting sights and smells. He lingered there, trying to imagine what all the delicacies would taste like.

"Well h-e-l-l-o there," said a syrupy voice.

Pooter looked up. Standing in the doorway was a lady as fluffy as a pink cloud. Her round rosy face was framed with silver ringlets, and she wore a large pink ruffled cap that matched her apron and dress. And when she spoke, her heart-shaped mouth moved like a little flower caught in the gentlest of breezes.

"Hungry, my little dear?" she cooed. "Who wouldn't be with all these goodies around, right, my sweets?"

What a kind, understanding lady, thought Pooter, getting ready for the handout of his life.

"Come inside and we'll see what little treat we have in store for you," she whispered enticingly.

"Oh yes, of course!" said Pooter, eager to set foot inside the marvelous confectionery.

Inside the shop there were baskets full of sweets everywhere—on the shelves, on the counters, and some even hung from the ceiling.

"I'll just have something from every basket," said Pooter. His eyes grew plate-sized.

"Now, where shall we start?" she said, giggling. "I'll bet you'd like something from every basket. A sampling of everything, right?"

Pooter wagged his tail and felt like rolling over with joy. "After all the terrible things that have happened, it's about time something good came my way," Pooter said, laughing.

"I think we'll have to start with something special," she said. "Now just you wait here!" The pink lady disappeared through a little doorway. At first Pooter thought she wouldn't fit through it, but she did, with great ease. Pooter was tempted to sample something in her absence, but he controlled himself and waited for her return.

When she did reappear, she had a large chocolate ball. It was so large that it required both of her hands to hold it.

"How is this for a bonbon?" she asked.

Never in all his life had Pooter seen a piece of candy that large. "It truly must be the largest piece of candy in the entire world," said Pooter.

As if playing a game of tenpins, she rolled the

candy to Pooter. He caught it in his mouth and took a big bite out of it at the same time.

"Oh goodie!" shouted the pink lady.

"Yum, yum, wow!" said Pooter, sinking his teeth deeper and deeper into the huge candy ball. Before he had a chance to finish it, Pooter found himself growing drowsy. What a time to get sleepy, he told himself. Then he stretched out and fell asleep.

The pink lady laughed quietly to herself.

"Andrew, Andrew! Come down. I'd like you to meet a friend of mine!" called Auntie Lizard.

"I don't feel like meeting any friend of yours," mumbled Andrew, but he obeyed.

As Andrew opened the door to leave, Jonas the cat left his post and preceded Andrew out of the room. Andrew followed the cat down the narrow winding stairway that led to the back of the shop.

When Andrew saw who Auntie Lizard's good friend was, his mouth opened in surprise. And Ashton Dansforth had the same reaction when he saw Andrew.

Observing their obvious expressions, Auntie Lizard asked, "Do you know each other?"

"Aunt Elizabeth, I don't know people like that, and I'm rather surprised you do," said Ashton Dansforth.

"Why Ashton, whatever do you mean?" said Auntie Lizard with concerned curiosity.

"Ask him, Auntie, just ask him," said Ashton Dansforth, folding his arms and looking up at the ceiling.

"What is going on here?" asked Auntie Lizard, turning toward Andrew for an answer.

At first Andrew didn't answer, then he stammered, "W-w-e met at the ferry."

"Met at the ferry indeed!" shouted Ashton Dansforth, outraged. "It is because of him, and that friend of his, that I nearly drowned in that storm last night. They plotted against me, and succeeded in making my arrival here a tardy one!"

Auntie Lizard drew herself close to Andrew. "Is that true? And who is your friend, and where is he now?" She asked her questions like a formidable judge eager to make a decision.

Andrew didn't like being interrogated in such a fierce manner. He thought Ashton's behavior had been awful, but he didn't want to bring that up because there was the risk of making things worse. And in his present position he didn't have any ally to back him up.

He felt an anger welling within himself, and he wanted to yell out loud and tell them both what he thought of them. But he resisted this temptation and said somberly, "He got what he deserved."

"And what is that supposed to mean?" interrupted Ashton Dansforth.

"You know what it means," said Andrew, who added a sardonic tone to his answer.

"Tell me, Andrew, who was this friend of yours?" pursued Auntie Lizard.

"His name is Peter Bronck and he was just on an errand to fetch Uncle Hendrick."

"Peter Bronck, a friend!" shrieked Auntie Lizard. She walked around the shop awhile and mumbled to herself. When she returned to Andrew she had regained her composure. "Andrew, darling," she began. "In life there are many pitfalls, therefore one must be very careful with whom one chooses to associate. I am certain, knowing what a bright boy you are, that if you had investigated the background of your supposed friend and this uncle of his, I won't even mention his name, you would recoil with repulsion as to their activities. Enough said! Now let us forget past events and begin anew. I'm sure you two could grow quite fond of one another."

Never! said Andrew to himself.

Jonas rubbed himself against Auntie Lizard's skirt.

"Now let's all be good pussycats," she said, lifting the cat and cradling him in her arms. "My little familiar," she whispered.

11

When Pooter awoke he found he was in a gloomy place where gray shadows were interwoven with black shadows. It was a place without any defined boundaries and yet there was a feeling of confinement. Pooter wanted to bark, but when he tried to, he merely yawned.

Where am I? Pooter asked himself, feeling very strange and not at all like himself. The last thing he remembered was the giant piece of candy. "It was so good," he said.

The pink lady appeared out of the shadows, like the moon from behind dark clouds on a starless night.

"Well, my dear, how are you?" she asked.

"Not very well, thanks to you," said Pooter.

The pink lady was carrying a large book and a sack full of things that rattled.

"I hope you are well and ready," she said.

"Ready?" said Pooter. "The only thing I'm ready for is getting out of this dreary place, wherever it is." When Pooter tried to move he soon realized that he had a chain around his neck that was securely fastened to the floor.

"You're not going anywhere just yet," said the pink lady. "You are just what I need for my little spell, I think."

"I don't want to be a part of any spell, and what's more, I'm not very good at them. As a matter of fact, I'm really rotten at them. I mean, I've ruined more good spells than you can shake a broomstick at."

"I'm sure you will cooperate, or else the results can be devastating." Her small lips twisted up into a sinister smile.

"I'll cooperate by biting your nose off," Pooter yelped. "Let me out of here!"

"No use spending your energy making noise. Anyway, the children can't hear you; they are busy at the ovens making all those wonderful things that led you to me."

"What children?" said Pooter. "I didn't see any children."

The pink lady removed an enormous bullfrog from her bag. "My little sweetheart familiar," she said, kissing the frog. "We are going to make magic, aren't we, my baby?" The pink lady kissed the frog again, only this time on his belly. "These new spells can be so tedious—trial and error, trial and error. But when the results can be so monumentally rewarding, it's all worth it!"

The pink lady swirled around and thrust her arms upward, wiggling her fingers. She turned around and around until she covered her mouth with her

hand. "I'm getting dizzy and nauseous," she exclaimed, falling to the floor.

"I was getting nauseous looking at you, lady. I
don't know if anyone has ever told you this, but you
are definitely not a dancer."

The pink lady sat on the ground, sighing heavily
and gasping for air. After a while she crawled on her
hands and knees to the sack and removed a crooked
stick from it. Then she began to draw a large triangle
around Pooter.

"I hope your artwork is better than your dancing," said Pooter, who was getting frightened by the
unusual amount of zeal with which the pink lady
approached her work.

The pink lady reached into her sack again. This
time she came up empty-handed and cried, "Damn!
Damn! Damn! I forgot the candles." The pink lady
moved away from Pooter and vanished into the
cloudy shadows.

"Stay put, my pets. I shall return!" she called out.

"Stay put? I have no choice! Where can I go with
this chain around my neck? I think it's cemented to
the floor." Pooter wanted to cry.

"We'll settle everything over a good meal," said
Auntie Lizard, taking complete control of the situation, as she was always capable of doing. "What shall
we have?"

Although Andrew didn't care for Auntie Lizard, down deep he couldn't help but admire the way she could always take over and get things going. It was something he felt he lacked, and he hoped that by the time he grew up he too could just take things over and be a kind of boss.

Auntie Lizard ran her fingers across her mouth as if it were a harmonica. "It will have to be something special. Why, this is practically a celebration!"

Celebration indeed! thought Andrew. I have nothing to celebrate. He didn't like the idea of having to eat with Ashton Dansforth and Auntie Lizard, but he hadn't any choice. There wasn't anyplace else to go to, and he was hungry—in fact so hungry, he told himself he would eat anything Auntie Lizard would prepare. He couldn't imagine her being a very good cook, and he was preparing himself for some foul-tasting stew.

"Let me fix the meal," said Ashton Dansforth with great enthusiasm.

"That's fine with me," said Auntie Lizard.

"Saved!" whispered Andrew. He thought anyone had to be a better cook than Auntie Lizard, though he did wonder just how much better Ashton Dansforth could be.

"You see, Andrew, when Ashton was your age—" She paused, and murmured, "That seems like only days ago."

From the expression in her eyes, Andrew could

tell Auntie Lizard had drifted backward into another time. She stayed there for a while and then returned to pick up the conversation where she had left off. "When Ashton was your age he came to spend the summer with me, and I taught him many things. Cooking was one of them."

"And I've been grateful to you ever since," said Ashton, winking and smiling.

It was a sneaky wink and a sly smile. Andrew got the impression that he was being left out of a joke; he felt like an outsider. Who'd want to share a joke with them, anyway? he told himself.

Auntie Lizard gently nudged Andrew toward the kitchen.

Andrew's stay up to that point had been like a game of blindman's buff without the blindfold. When he first arrived, Andrew was ushered through the dark shop and taken to his room. He could only get the impression of a mysterious-looking place with exotic fragrances, a place that he was eager to explore.

The kitchen was a small crowded room with a fireplace at one end. Cupboards and tables were stacked high with pots, pans, plates, cups, crocks, colanders, and bowls. The ceiling was hung with wooden spoons, and forks, rolling pins, graters, mashers, and spices decorated the walls like a stenciled pattern.

Andrew couldn't help but feel it was a place

where things happened. Good or bad, he would know soon enough.

Moving around the room like a soup green caught in a boil, Auntie Lizard exclaimed, "Oh, Andrew, cooking is such an art!"

Ashton Dansforth bowed his head in agreement.

"A well-prepared meal may be one of life's more magical experiences!" she continued. "Isn't that true, my dear Jonas?" The orange cat remained fixed in Auntie Lizard's arms, only moving his tongue across his mouth.

"I'll conjure up something wonderful," said Ashton Dansforth. Removing his coat and throwing it aside, he rolled up his sleeves and put an apron on.

"Wonderful and quick," said Auntie Lizard. "We are all starving!"

"It will be my surprise!" cried Ashton, rushing around the kitchen gathering up utensils.

"And for dessert we'll get something from Celestial Grace's Confectionery Shop," said Auntie Lizard. She reached into a little leather pouch and handed Andrew some money. "Get us some sweet things," she instructed.

As Andrew bounded out the door, Auntie Lizard shouted the way there, and Ashton called out, "Get something magnificent. We won't settle for anything less!"

"He would make it a difficult task," Andrew said as he made his way there.

The confectionery shop was an easy place to find—he just had to follow his nose. The smells that greeted him inside the shop made him want everything.

"Perhaps it won't be so difficult a task after all," said Andrew, inspecting the baskets full of goodies. "Everything looks magnificent!"

A girl about the same age as Andrew appeared from the back of the shop. "Can I be of any help?" she inquired shyly.

Andrew wanted to laugh when he saw her. She was covered from head to foot with flour. He was unable to control himself, and he said laughingly, "If I didn't know any better, I'd say that you were a ghost."

"I don't think that's very funny," she said quietly, but loud enough for Andrew to hear.

"I'm sorry," said Andrew, feeling a little bad. He knew he had hurt the girl's feelings.

"What is it you would like?" she asked again.

"Everything!" teased Andrew.

"Everything?" answered the girl, surprised.

"Yes, I would like everything, but I'm going to buy dessert for only three people, and one of them is me. I'm Andrew Van Aken."

The girl was joined by four other children, two

girls, and two boys, all younger and looking like ghosts also.

"If Miss Grace finds us all out here, she will be very angry," warned the older girl.

"Miss Grace is very angry!" scolded the pink lady, who seemed to appear from out of nowhere. "How many times do I have to tell you, your place is at the ovens!"

The children quickly disappeared. "Now, young man, what is it that you want?" Miss Grace asked impatiently. She tapped her fingers on the counter.

Andrew made his choice quickly, eager to get away from the pink lady, who frightened him.

As he left, she placed a SHOP CLOSED sign in the window.

Andrew sensed that there was something strange about Miss Grace and the children, but he couldn't figure out what it was.

12

"Now where are those candles?" said Miss Grace, searching frantically through her candle boxes marked SPECIAL CANDLES FOR MY USE ONLY!

Exasperated by her futile hunt, she approached the children. "Have you seen my black candles?" she asked wearily.

"The ones in the boxes?" answered Prunella, the eldest.

"Yes, those!" said Miss Grace, her eyes opening sunflower size. "Where are they?"

"We've been using them," said the girl politely. "We told you weeks ago, miss, that we had run out of lamp oil."

"Using them!" screeched Miss Celestial Grace. "Can't you read what it says on the boxes?"

"No, Miss Grace," answered the girl in a gentle, trembling voice. "You have never allowed us to learn how to read."

Under her breath Miss Celestial Grace said, "When I complete my new spell no one will be able to read. I'll render everyone powerless!"

Celestial Grace shook her warning finger and

spoke through clenched teeth. "From now on you and your family will stay away from my personal property! Do you all understand?"

The children huddled together, quivering. They were terrified of Miss Grace and her stormlike temper. They kept nodding yes.

"Get back to your chores!" she commanded harshly. "I smell a pie burning!"

The children returned to the hot, airless baking room and went unhappily about their chores. Sifting flour, kneading, and rolling the dough. Pitting cherries, peaches, plums, and apricots. Stirring, churning, and mixing.

"I wish Miss Grace had never adopted us," said Peachum, the second eldest.

"So do I." Pearetta, the youngest sister, sighed.

"Unfortunately, we hadn't any choice," said Prunella glumly. "No one else wanted all five of us. The important thing is that we are all together."

"I suppose so," said Plumwell, the older brother. "But I sometimes think things would have been better at an orphanage."

"At least we'd get to play, and we'd probably eat better also," complained Appleton, the youngest.

"He's right," said Peachum. "We are never even allowed to taste what we bake. It's always crumbs and leftovers."

"All we ever do is work, work, work!" said Plumwell, cutting a large round piecrust.

"Things will get better," said Prunella. "I hope!"
She sighed.

In her room Celestial Grace pulled a book from
under her bed. "Now I'll have to make new candles," she mumbled, thumbing through her *Witches'
Arts Manual.* She turned to where it said "Candle
Making for Spells and Curses."

Using her finger as a pointer, she read aloud.
" 'Needed: wax from the ears of a dwarf.' Do I
know any waxy-eared dwarfs?" she mused.

Andrew returned to the apothecary shop and
made his way to the kitchen. There wasn't anyone
there. An open doorway in the kitchen framed a
sunny, leafy garden.

"We're here! We're here!" Auntie Lizard and
Ashton called out.

Andrew stepped out into a small garden. It was
crisscrossed by brick paths and boxed in by a beech
arbor. A festive table was set in the center where the
paths crossed.

"Welcome to my botanical nature garden," said
Auntie Lizard.

"And here is our courier with the dessert," said
Ashton, relieving Andrew of the package and peer-
ing into it. "Oh, what wonderful treats!" he cried,

and practically danced back to the kitchen. "Don't anyone leave!" he shouted. "We shall be feasting shortly."

"Come, sit here!" said Auntie Lizard, motioning for Andrew to come to the table.

Andrew sat down next to Auntie Lizard. In her garden surroundings Auntie Lizard was transformed into a different person. Here she was someone tender, understanding, and almost motherly.

She inquired at length about his family, and surprised Andrew by asking about Pooter. Then she told him how really delighted she was by his visit. And promised him a good time.

"There are many things you'll learn here," said Auntie Lizard, gently touching Andrew on his head.

"So many things indeed!" said Ashton Dansforth, reappearing in the garden with a tray full of unusual and decorative-looking things to eat. "Did you tell him about the crescent moon party?" he said, placing the tray on the table.

"Crescent moon party?" asked Andrew.

"Yes, that's one of the reasons I'm here," said Ashton. "Aunt Elizabeth took me to one when I was your age. It was my very first, just as this will be yours. It changed my whole life." He smiled. "And do you know, I haven't missed one since."

"I've never heard of a crescent moon party!" exclaimed Andrew.

"Before the summer is over, dear boy, there'll be

many things you'll be hearing about," said Ashton.

"And seeing too!" Auntie Lizard chuckled.

Andrew grew impatient. He still didn't know what a crescent moon party was. He knew about birthday parties, and holiday parties, but this was a party he had never heard about before.

"What is a crescent moon party?" he asked with determination.

At first Auntie Lizard was somewhat flustered, but then she said, "It's a celebration of the crescent summer moon. A rite that is peculiar to just the inhabitants of Wiltwyck Landing. Its origin is somewhat shrouded in time, but we've been doing it for years, and since everyone has such a good time, we will not question or abandon it."

"You'll have a wonderful time," said Ashton. "And you'll get to wear a costume."

"A costume?" said Andrew.

"Yes," said Ashton. "It's sort of a preview of Halloween."

"But Halloween is so far away," said Andrew.

"I know," said Ashton. "But why wait for good times? You've got to make them happen!"

"Oh, Ashton, you are a marvel in the kitchen," said Auntie Lizard, eyeing the table full of food.

"Oh thank you, Aunt Elizabeth, you are much too kind," said Ashton, glowing with pride. Then he looked at Andrew. "Help yourself," he said, lifting a platter full of clams elaborately garnished with parsley, ferns, and lemons.

Andrew sat with his arms folded.

"Is there something wrong?" Auntie Lizard inquired.

"If clams aren't to your liking," said Ashton, "there are snails with lots of garlic!"

"Oh, I love snails," swooned Auntie Lizard.

The thought of snails made Andrew lose his hunger.

"Have some squabs," said Ashton. He held high a skewer full of small roasted birds. "Or perhaps you'd like liver sausage, my own recipe. I've added tons of freshly ground oregano to them."

Auntie Lizard leaned over the table. She cupped her hand to her mouth and took on a secretive air. "No one can resist liver sausage with oregano—it's the treat of treats, especially with mushrooms. That's my idea," she whispered.

Not wanting to hurt anyone's feelings, and realizing that he had to eat something, Andrew tasted the food. To his surprise, he thought it was all very good.

"Once you sample Ashton's kitchen wizardry, you'll be clamoring for more," said Auntie Lizard, picking at a squab and appearing for a moment like a large scavenger bird.

When Andrew reached for seconds, Ashton said,

"Good lad!" He appeared to be pleased with Andrew and himself.

During the meal Auntie Lizard and Ashton talked about many things, at times almost forgetting that Andrew was in their presence.

They spoke of long-ago times. Ashton told of the many people he had met and the portraits he had painted. He broke off his conversation and looked at Andrew. "Perhaps I will paint your portrait."

Andrew suddenly grew uncomfortable, and he didn't know how to respond. He wasn't quite sure if Ashton really meant it, or whether it was just a way of paying some attention to him.

"Wouldn't that be wonderful?" said Auntie Lizard. She reached her arm across the table and touched Andrew's face.

Andrew felt his face grow red.

"He'll be a wonderful subject," said Ashton.

Andrew was glad when the topic of conversation turned away from him. He had grown uncomfortable being the focus of their attention.

Their conversation resumed, with Ashton telling Auntie Lizard that he was running low on supplies. She told him not to worry—she would remedy that.

Andrew was surprised to hear that Ashton Dansforth was able to get his art supplies at Auntie Lizards'. But then again, Andrew realized he hadn't even explored the apothecary shop yet.

Quite a few times during the course of their lively

conversation, Ashton would say, "Oh, dear Aunt Elizabeth, you've been such an influence on my life." And at one point he said, "You've truly made me what I am today."

Andrew found it difficult to believe that Auntie Lizard had taught him how to paint. What else could he be referring to? Andrew thought.

13

The desserts that followed tasted even better than Andrew had imagined.

And Ashton was generous with his praise. "If exquisite jewels were transformed into desserts, they would certainly take on the look and taste of these pastries." He savored every bite.

Andrew was in complete agreement with him, and he wanted to say something about the young girl who worked there, but he didn't.

Much to his surprise, Auntie Lizard brought the subject up. "It's those children of hers. They're not her real children—adopted you know—" Auntie Lizard was interrupted by the tinkling of a bell that hung in the shop. "Now who could that be?" she said, raising herself from her chair.

She excused herself and left the garden. "Speak of the d— I mean we were just speaking about you," she said. "It's Miss Celestial Grace!" Auntie Lizard spoke in a forced loud voice. Andrew was positive it was for the benefit of Ashton and himself. After a while Auntie Lizard lowered her voice and Andrew was unable to hear anything.

"Miss Celestial Grace has a dog tied up in the supply cellar," said Plumwell and Peachum.

"A dog!" cried the other children.

"What would she be doing with a dog?" asked Prunella.

"Oh, let's go down and see him," said Pearetta and Appleton.

"What if she catches us?" said Prunella.

"We could just tell her that we had to get more flour. That's how we discovered him in the first place," said Plumwell.

The children approached the supply cellar with caution.

"Do you think he bites?" asked Appleton.

"He really looked quite harmless," said Peachum. "As a matter of fact, I really feel very sorry for him."

"So do I," said Plumwell.

The children unlocked the wide plank door and went in.

Pooter jumped up and down, happy to see them.

"Please untie me," he said.

Prunella, the eldest and the bravest, went right up

to Pooter. "What are you doing here?" she asked, stroking his head.

"Run for your lives, children! I'm here because that harmless-looking pink lady is a witch. She's out to do everyone in by working a spell so everyone will forget how to read. I know what I'm talking about. She gave me a sleeping potion. For some reason I'm needed for the spell, or she thinks she needs me. Anyway, run, I warn you! And take me with you, PLEASE!"

"Shall we let him go?" asked Prunella. "He looks so uncomfortable."

"I am uncomfortable," sighed Pooter.

"If we let him go Miss Grace will know for sure that we did it. Then she will be really angry, and you know what that will mean," said Plumwell.

"Do you think she got him as a surprise for us?" asked Appleton, touching Pooter also.

"No, I'm no surprise," said Pooter. "The only surprise is what she is up to, and I know it's not going to be a good one."

"He's the saddest-looking dog I've ever seen," said Prunella.

"You'd be sad also if you were miles away from home. A witch's prisoner who is using you for some awful spell. Oh, let me go. I've never harmed anyone in my whole life. I must admit I have chased a few rabbits, but I don't deserve this fate," he moaned.

Prunella left Pooter's side and took a position near the door. "I'd better stand guard and listen for Miss Grace's return."

"I think he's hungry," said Pearetta.

"I am hungry," said Pooter. "And scared, too!"

"Appleton, you're the smallest. Make your way quickly upstairs and bring something down for this poor creature," said Prunella. "And be on the alert for Miss Grace."

Appleton hurried upstairs.

"I wonder how wise it was to send Appleton," said Plumwell. "You know how clumsy he can be."

"We hadn't any other choice," said Prunella. "He can move about the shop unnoticed—or practically unnoticed."

"I sure hope he hurries," said Peachum. "I'm getting nervous."

"Just untie me and let me go," said Pooter. "I promise I won't tell Witch Whatever-Her-Name-Is who did it. As a matter of fact, I'll never go near her again," Pooter cried.

Thumping noises came from the shop. "What is going on up there?" asked Prunella. "I'm beginning to think this whole thing is a mistake."

"You can say that again," said Pooter.

Appleton returned with an armful of cookies.

"Good work," they said when they saw him.

"What was all that thumping?" asked Prunella.

"A basket full of sweet rolls fell on the floor," said Appleton. "But I put them back carefully."

Just as they were about to feed the cookies to Pooter, Prunella whispered, "I think I hear Miss Grace turning the key in the front door."

The children quickly left the cellar, leaving Pooter once again alone in the dark.

Auntie Lizard returned to the garden. "It was Celestial Grace," she said. "She placed an order. One of my best customers, you know. When I get it filled, you'll deliver it, Andrew. I must say her orders are rather demanding," said Auntie Lizard under her breath. "I have a feeling this time she's onto something big."

Auntie Lizard took her place at the table. Her face had a troubled expression.

Andrew wasn't the only one who noticed it. Because Ashton spoke up and said, "Is everything all right?"

There was a long silence before an answer came, and when it did, it seemed as if Auntie Lizard wasn't sure of a positive response.

"Now, what were we discussing before business intruded?" she asked.

"While you were gone Andrew was concerned that he didn't have any costume to wear to the crescent moon party. I told him not to worry, because we have a wonderful costume for him. Don't we?''

Ashton took great delight in any discussion pertaining to the crescent moon party. That subject brought a certain amount of color to his unusually pale complexion.

Auntie Lizard was truly harboring a worry. With forced joviality she said, "Oh, we'll have a grand time, and it's only a few days away."

Ashton told Auntie Lizard that he would be leaving that evening, but that she could count on him to return in plenty of time for the party.

"Oh dear!" cried Auntie Lizard. "I almost forgot to serve tea. That's my specialty. It's a very special secret blend, pure ambrosia, my dears, pure ambrosia!"

Queenlike, Auntie Lizard swept her way regally into the kitchen.

A warm honey-colored afternoon light filtered through the beech arbor. The garden was patterned as if covered by a large lacy shawl. A sweet tingly perfume drifted toward the syrupy light. Andrew closed his eyes and imagined himself to be floating.

Ashton Dansforth observed Andrew, his lips turned upward in a smile. It was as if he knew what Andrew was experiencing. "Herbs," he whispered. "Wonderful, tantalizing herbs, sweet, giving herbs; when properly used their effects are infinite. Rosemary, coriander, and thyme."

It was difficult for Andrew to keep his eyes open. He found himself growing drowsy.

Auntie Lizard came out of the kitchen with Jonas wrapped around her neck. "Teatime, teatime," she announced.

The drowsy feeling increased and Andrew found staying awake an almost impossible task.

"Poor Andrew, he's exhausted," said Auntie Lizard, setting down the teapot.

"I'm sorry, I'm so sleepy . . ." were the last words Andrew said before Ashton and Auntie Lizard carried him off to bed.

14

When Andrew was comfortably tucked into bed, Auntie Lizard and Ashton returned to the garden and their tea.

"Do you think he suspects anything?" asked Ashton.

"I don't think so," said Auntie Lizard, stirring her tea.

"If he had spent any more time with that Peter Bronck, it is very conceivable that things would have gone awry." Ashton carefully measured the amount of cream he poured into his tea.

"Fortunately the crescent moon rite isn't too far off, and then he will be one of us." Auntie Lizard sighed deeply.

"On what pretext did you get him away from his family?" questioned Ashton.

"On a rather feeble one, I'm afraid. I told them I was in poor health and in need of help. I do wish I had been more imaginative."

"It was our good fortune that they were willing to relinquish a healthy lad from his summer chores."

Ashton looked over the rim of his cup and arched his brows.

"They hadn't any choice; it was the fulfillment of a long-ago commitment." Auntie Lizard became reflective. "Andrew was a sickly infant. His condition became a matter of life and death. I was sent for, and needless to say I saved his life. Therefore the deep obligation. I have always maintained contact with the family. My owning an apothecary shop is a natural excuse for me to be there with the right treatment in times of ill health. And of course keep watch on my budding—what shall I say?—apprentice."

Auntie Lizard and Ashton giggled while emptying their cups of the last drops of tea.

"Apprentice?" said Ashton.

"I never cared for the word warlock," she said. "I think it conjures up an awful image."

"Neither have I, I must confess, but that's what I am, and that's what I'm called, and I suppose I'm just stuck with it." Ashton's voice was tinged with hopeless resignation. "Anyway, dear Elizabeth, as we know, titles mean nothing; it's what we do that's important."

"True, true," exclaimed Auntie Lizard, refilling the empty cups. "With our dwindling numbers, it is most urgent that we get a new member into our ranks." Auntie Lizard grew pensive. "I'm afraid the secretive nature of our lot prevents us from meeting others. Therefore the marriage rate is low, and reproduction is almost nonexistent. Thus true-born witches are rare. As we know, though, through hard work and great determination many things are possible."

"Yes, we are the hard-working variety," said Ashton. "By the way, what did Celestial Grace want?"

"Now there is a true-born witch, unlike ourselves," said Auntie Lizard. "Her power is vast, and she is up to something. Something that has me worried."

"Worried?"

"Yes, because I have a feeling she is onto something that will affect many, including you and me. Of course it's just a feeling, but nevertheless, I don't want to underestimate that woman's intentions. I truly think she was responsible for that storm last night, and I also suspect it was she who deviously managed to get Uncle Hendrick away."

"So you think it was she who pulled the spell on the other side of the river?" asked Ashton.

"I would be inclined to say yes. His departure left the way for her to operate freely." Auntie Lizard tapped her spoon anxiously on the empty cup. "What has really got me worried is her request for the ingredients necessary for the making of black candles."

"Black candles!" cried Ashton. "She must be up to something really big. Do you think we could spy without her knowing?"

Auntie Lizard stroked Jonas. "That's exactly what I was thinking!" She raised her eyes upward toward Andrew's room. "He's the one to do it. She will never suspect Andrew of spying. And we will plan it in such a way that he will be unaware of his mission."

"Wonderful idea," said Ashton. "But do you think it is wise to send him before he is initiated? He will be totally powerless if she should catch on to him."

"I don't think we have the time. She seemed quite urgent." Auntie Lizard paused. "Of course, you realize my assumption is all totally speculative, and Celestial Grace could be engaged in some harmless little maneuver. But judging from her past performances, and my usually infallible instincts: She's up to no good!"

Auntie Lizard emptied the teapot of its leaves and spread them out on the table.

"Our future is waiting to be read," she announced.

"Oh, let me read them," said Ashton.

Celestial Grace grew impatient fidgeting with her key and the front-door lock, which was stuck. She put the key away and went directly through the keyhole.

When she got into the shop she called for the children. Rage colored her voice. "Children, come here!" she screamed.

The children quickly obeyed.

"What's going on here?" she asked.

"What do you mean?" asked Prunella.

"What do I mean? That front-door lock is what I mean! Who's been tampering with it?"

Appleton grew red. When he had been upstairs searching the shop for food, he had secured the lock to make sure they wouldn't be interrupted when feeding the dog.

"Is there something you have to tell me?" she asked.

Little Appleton began to cry.

"Why the tears, small one?" Celestial Grace shook him. "Stop your sniveling, and talk!"

"We weren't doing anything," said Plumwell.

"I wasn't asking you," she said, giving him one of her meanest looks. Celestial Grace lifted Appleton high into the air. "Tell me what you were up to, or I will shake it out of you."

"We were only feeding the dog," he cried.

"Only feeding the dog!" she screamed. "Punishment for all of you!"

Celestial Grace ran into her room. "This is a bad

day for bad witches. Now I'll have to find another dog—that one has been contaminated by the children's touch. I'll have to get rid of him!"

Ashton followed Auntie Lizard into the apothecary shop. She lit a lamp and went behind a counter. There she searched for a book, and when she found the right one she placed it on the counter top. It was a large, worn, leatherbound edition of *Plots and Plans.*

"Now, let us find a good clever plot for Andrew so he may observe Celestial Grace undetected." Auntie Lizard turned the pages, muttering to herself, "Mmm, they're all so obvious and detectable. Peephole spying, indeed!" She briskly turned the page.

"He could pretend to be a plant," said Ashton.

"Too immobile," said Auntie Lizard.

"You're probably right," said Ashton.

"Oh, this book is so outdated," said Auntie Lizard, slamming it shut and waving away the dust that flew when she did it.

"Perhaps we should proceed along lines that are more pertinent to the situation," said Ashton.

"Such as?" asked Auntie Lizard.

"Well, we could send him on the ruse that we would like the recipe for the ginger tart. It would solve two problems," said Ashton.

"What two problems?"

"I would truly like to get the recipe for the tart, and it will allow Andrew to get into the shop and do some investigative work." Ashton seemed very pleased with his idea.

"Oh Ashton, you are a clever boy!" shouted Auntie Lizard. "First thing in the morning, Andrew shall begin his apprenticeship."

"I certainly hope he carries it off well," said Ashton.

"I hope so," sighed Auntie Lizard, "for all our sakes!"

Then Ashton told Auntie Lizard he would have to be leaving soon, and that he did need supplies. "For deep spells and light trances."

15

A gloom settled over the Van Aken household. With both Andrew and Pooter gone, things weren't the same.

Meg accused Ellen of being a traitor when she suggested that they get another dog. "Pooter's got to come back," she cried.

When they couldn't sleep at night, and Mrs. Van Aken asked why, the girls said, "It's too hot!"

But their mother and father knew better. Hoping to cheer the girls up, Farmer Van Aken suggested that he build them a tree house, so that they could sleep in the leafy cool of night.

Ellen said, "What fun is a tree house without Andrew and Pooter to share it?"

Meg agreed with her sister.

In spite of his daughters' attitude, Farmer Van Aken went ahead with his plans for a tree house, hoping that when it was completed the children would feel differently about it. It also gave the farmer something new to do, something to keep his mind off Andrew and Pooter.

Mrs. Van Aken spoke hopefully of the time Andrew and Pooter would return, and how they would have a party.

She engaged the girls in helping her plan an imaginary party. But when Meg and Ellen were alone, they said, "I wonder if we ever will have a party?"

Pooter snarled as Celestial Grace returned to the supply cellar.

"Oh, quiet!" snapped Miss Grace. "Those children have ruined my spell. They spoiled it all by seeing and touching you. Secrecy is of the utmost when preparing an important spell such as mine. Now I'll have to dispose of you in a clever way."

"Dispose of me!" said Pooter. "What does she think I am, a piece of garbage? I'd like to dispose of her with a good chomp or two. The indigestion I'd get would be well worth it."

"How shall I get rid of you?" Celestial Grace circled around, shaking her head from side to side. Her curls shook beneath her cap. "Perhaps there is a profit to be made by your removal," she muttered. "A visit to Professor Effingham Humphries, the noted inventor, will solve my problems."

Celestial Grace shook herself, at first gently, and then the shaking became more agitated.

Pooter watched in amazement as Celestial Grace shook off her physical appearance and was transformed into a charred old beggar.

"Things aren't always as they seem," she said, laughing.

Pooter tried desperately to free himself. But it was no use. The beggar came swooping down upon Pooter with a large sack, and Pooter was soon wriggling in the sack.

With the sack over his shoulder, the beggar left by the back door. The witch-beggar made his way out of the village by using a seldom-traveled footpath overgrown with prickly vines and spearlike weeds.

"What next?" Pooter thought as he lay upside down in the sack.

Ashton Dansforth bid Auntie Lizard good-bye. His bags were heavy with replenished supplies. "Hope everything goes well," he said.

"I hope so," said Auntie Lizard. "Apprentices are hard to come by."

"See you in time for the crescent moon," said Ashton, and he made his way into the fragrant summer night.

The cheerful sounds of morning pulled Andrew from his dreams. Dreams of home. When he awoke in the unfamiliar room, Andrew had the feeling that he had moved on to another dream. It took a little while of remembering for Andrew to know where he was.

The skillet rattled on the stove in the kitchen, and the birds visiting the beech arbor called to each other. Morning sounds hold promises, as all beginning things do. Andrew jumped from the bed, eager to discover what the day held in store. He told himself to look upon his stay at Auntie Lizard's not as a punishment, as he had originally thought, but as an adventure. He was looking forward to the crescent moon party; parties were fun.

Auntie Lizard placed a large kettle of water on the stove and rubbed some lard in the skillet. Jonas wove a circle around her hem, purring.

"I think I hear Andrew stirring," she said. "We've got a big day ahead of us, my pussums."

Andrew washed his face in the bowl alongside his bed. The water in the big pitcher was cool, and it felt good. He dressed and went downstairs into the kitchen.

"Good morning," he said.

Auntie Lizard greeted him cheerily. "Good morning, dear. Have a good sleep?" she asked.

"Oh yes, I slept wonderfully well, thank you," said Andrew. "I don't even remember going to sleep. I really must have been tired."

"You were, my dear, you were!"

Andrew looked around expecting to see Ashton Dansforth.

"Looking for Ashton?" asked Auntie Lizard. "He had to leave, but he will return in time for the party.

He did ask a favor of you," said Auntie Lizard, breaking some eggs into a skillet. "You do like eggs?"

"What kind of favor?" asked Andrew.

"Just a little one. We'll talk about it after breakfast. Nothing makes sense on an empty stomach."

All during breakfast Andrew could think of nothing but what the favor was that Ashton wanted.

After breakfast Andrew followed Auntie Lizard into the apothecary shop. It was a small, crowded place. In the center there was a counter that ran the length of the shop. Shelves crammed with various-sized boxes and bottles covered the walls. Roots, dried animal skins, and bones hung from the ceiling.

Andrew felt as if he were entering the secret closet of a traveling magician. It was the feeling of experiencing something special.

Jonas made his way over the counter top. Climbing on books and boxes, he walked assuredly on what appeared to be a well-traveled route, which ended in the arms of Auntie Lizard.

"Cures for all ills," said Auntie Lizard, waving one arm and twirling around the shop. "And ills for all cures," she whispered into the cat's ear.

Auntie Lizard danced around the room. "We have cures for bad breath, bunions, burns, corns, croup, dandruff, dyspepsia, diarrhea, earache, freckles. . . .' Her voice trailed off as she continued whirling toplike around the shop.

Andrew tried to read the labels on the bottles and boxes. "Deretla sevren, ehca fo eht niarb, elbatirri retcarahc, ytisebo. It doesn't make sense!" he said.

"That's because it's all backward," said Auntie Lizard.

"Backward?" exclaimed Andrew, surprised by this discovery.

"Yes, that's because I'm left-handed," said Auntie Lizard.

"So am I," said Andrew, "but I don't write backward."

"Oh, you are left-handed — how wonderful!" shrieked Auntie Lizard.

"Why is that wonderful?" asked Andrew, startled by Auntie Lizard's response.

"It just makes things easier."

"Easier?" Andrew repeated the word questioningly.

Auntie Lizard wore a huge grin. "Let us say it makes us more compatible."

The small bell on the door jingled. A turnip-shaped lady waddled into the shop. "Morning, Miss Hardwell." The woman spoke in a raspy voice.

"Good morning, Miss Hennipin," said Auntie Lizard. "Andrew, this is Miss Hennipin."

Andrew nodded his head. "Pleased to know you, ma'am," he said.

"Andrew is my new apprentice."

Miss Hennipin giggled. "Shall we be seeing him at our annual party?"

"But of course!" said Auntie Lizard. "He's looking forward to it, aren't you, Andrew?"

Andrew nodded in agreement. But he was beginning to wonder about what kind of party it was going to be with someone like Miss Hennipin there. She certainly didn't look like she'd be too much fun.

"Now, what can I do for you today?" asked Auntie Lizard.

Miss Hennipin struggled with a little cloth sack from which she removed a crumpled piece of paper. She put it down on the counter and tried to press out the wrinkles.

"Let me see." She pushed her face close to the paper and mumbled, "Spirits of hartshorn, spikenard, and a take of horehound."

Auntie Lizard scurried around the shop gathering up the things for Miss Hennipin. When they were all collected, she told Andrew to wrap them.

At first he had some trouble, but then he tied them all together in a neat little package. Andrew felt proud.

Auntie Lizard and Miss Hennipin said, "What a neat package."

"And he's left-handed too," announced Auntie Lizard proudly.

"You are!" said Miss Hennipin. "Isn't that nice."

At home, being left-handed was something of a

problem, especially at mealtimes. Elbows were always against each other. What had always been a
problem for Andrew was now considered something special.

Before she left, Miss Hennipin giggled and said,
"Have you noticed your new assistant also has green
eyes?"

Auntie Lizard drew herself close to Andrew.
"Why, he does!" She cackled making this discovery.
"It's all too perfect," she said.

"Too perfect for what?" asked Andrew.

"It's something we'll discuss later," said Auntie
Lizard.

Andrew figured if Auntie Lizard continued putting things off for later, a discussion would take
place that would last for weeks. Andrew brought up
the topic of the favor Ashton wanted of him.

"Oh dear!" screamed Auntie Lizard. "I almost
forgot, and it's terribly important."

"Important!" said Andrew.

"Well, important to Ashton," said Auntie Lizard.

She then proceeded to tell Andrew what was
wanted of him.

16

Pooter thought the bumpy trip inside the sack would never end. He had always considered himself rather flexible and athletic, but this trip was a totally new experience that required the talents of a contortionist. His body and head ached from the impossible positions he was forced into.

"Upside down is definitely no way to travel," he told himself.

The trip ended with a thud. Overcome with dizziness, Pooter lay still in the sack. He wondered where he was and if this was the journey's end. Then he heard voices. He recognized the voice of the witch.

"I've brought you a good dog this time," said the witch.

"That's what you said the other time, and the dog didn't last but a day."

"Oh no, I can assure you this dog is of a hardier breed."

Pooter was scared. "I wonder how much longer I'm going to be able to hold out," he said.

"You know I need a strong dog for my invention."

"This one is strong," said the witch.

"All right, let me take a look at it."

Pooter was removed from the sack. The witch held him by the scruff of the neck. A pale bony man in a long white frock coat pushed his face close to Pooter. The man wore two sets of spectacles and examined Pooter closely. After a lot of sniffing and grumbling, he said somewhat reluctantly, "Not the best, but he'll do." Then he looked at the witch and asked, "How much do you want for him?"

Pooter groaned, "I'm being sold like a bolt of cloth. This is the final straw!" He began to growl.

"Better not act up," said the man in the frock coat. "I know how to deal with mongrels."

Pooter snapped at the insult.

"Don't you snap at Professor Effingham Humphries. I am the world-famous inventor, and you shall be put to work for me. A rare privilege for an ordinary dog."

The professor put a muzzle and a harness on Pooter, and then completed his business with the witch.

"Good-bye, dog," said the charred old witch.

"We've got work to do," said the professor, rubbing his hands together.

Andrew listened as Auntie Lizard told him that he should go to Celestial Grace's Confectionery Shop.

"Befriend the children and try to get the recipe for the ginger tart." Auntie Lizard hemmed and hawed, and then she said, "And see if there is anything unusual afoot there."

The latter part of the request surprised Andrew.

Auntie Lizard read Andrew's expression. She said, "Oh, it's just that Celestial Grace is sometimes a troublemaker of sorts. And I just thought that perhaps the children would know what she is up to. You see, last year she wasn't invited to the crescent moon party, and she has been doing all sorts of terrible things ever since. Andrew, she is a revengeful person. Keep your inquiries away from her. But at the same time, remember they should be about her."

Andrew realized that he was being asked to spy. At first the idea seemed like fun, but then he remembered from his history lessons that spies, when caught, were hanged. He told himself he wouldn't get caught.

When Andrew returned to the bakeshop, the children greeted him happily. From this reception it was obvious to Andrew that Celestial Grace wasn't around.

"And how are you today, Andrew Van Aken?" asked Prunella.

Andrew was flattered that she remembered his name. "You are all at an advantage," he said. "I don't know your names."

"I'm Prunella."

"I'm Peachum."

"I'm Pearetta."

"Hello, I'm Plumwell."

"And I'm Appleton."

"I've never heard names like that before," said Andrew.

"Our parents named us after fruits," said Prunella. "They were wonderful bakers, and they loved fruit fillings."

"They loved us too, until they died," said Peachum.

"They taught us how to bake," said Pearetta.

"How did you end up here?" asked Andrew.

"It was either an orphanage or splitting us up," said Prunella.

"Celestial Grace heard about our baking ability and took us all. She opened this shop, and that's all we've been doing ever since." Peachum spoke, holding back a cry.

"We can never do anything we want to," said Plumwell. "Miss Grace says that children don't have any rights."

"She hates all children," said Appleton.

"She even hates our names," said Peachum.

"That's because she hates fruits," said Prunella. "She is allergic to them."

"I'm allergic to her," said Plumwell. "She always gives me a bad case of the shakes."

"The shakes?" said Andrew.

"Yes, every time she hollers, we all shake," said Appleton.

Andrew felt very sorry for the children. He wished he could say "Come live with me and my family." Trying to comfort them, he did say, "Things will get better."

"What would you like today?" asked Prunella.

"I don't want to buy anything," said Andrew, "but I would like the recipe for the ginger tart."

"Well, first you take some flour, and then add—"

Andrew interrupted Prunella. "I'm sorry, I forgot to take a pencil and paper with me. Can you please write it down?"

"I can't write," said Prunella.

"You can't write?" said Andrew, surprised.

"None of us can," said Plumwell. "And we can't read either!"

"Celestial Grace doesn't want anyone to read or write," said Peachum.

"Except herself," said Appleton.

"She's always reading from some big old book," said Pearetta.

"And after she reads from it, she always gathers up things," said Plumwell.

"What kind of things?" asked Andrew.

"Strange things," said Prunella.

Andrew found himself becoming interested in Celestial Grace's behavior.

"She just got a dog," said Appleton.

"And it's not for a pet," said Prunella.

"She has it in the storage room," said Appleton. "Do you want to see it?"

Andrew thought of Pooter and wished he could see him soon again. "Sure, I'd like to see it. I have a dog back home," he said.

In his eagerness to see the dog, Andrew put aside precautions and followed the children down into the storage room.

They opened the door slowly, and were surprised to find the room empty.

"Where do you think he's gone to?" asked Plumwell.

"She must have taken him with her when she left," said Prunella.

"He was tied right here," said Appleton, running to where Pooter had been.

The children all wondered what had happened to the dog, and what Celestial Grace was doing with it.

"Poor dog, wherever he is," said Andrew.

"She is always up to something," said Peachum. "We just never know what she is doing."

"She never tells us a thing," said Plumwell.

"Except what we haven't done, and what we must do," said Prunella.

"We had better get out of here before she returns," said Peachum.

"Good idea!" said Andrew, who was beginning

to grow fidgety being someplace he felt he shouldn't be.

Upstairs in the shop, Andrew was about to say good-bye when Prunella said, "Don't you want the ginger tart recipe?"

"Yes," said Andrew. "I will return with a writing pad and pencil."

Auntie Lizard wasn't about when Andrew returned to her shop. She didn't respond to the sound of the bell, or to Andrew's calling her.

Andrew went behind the counter searching for a writing pad and pencil. While searching, he came across two books, *The Good Witches' Manual of Ordinary Spells* and *The Bad Witches' Manual of Extraordinary Spells.*

Andrew was startled by Auntie Lizard's choice of reading matter. He quickly pushed away any suspicious and unpleasant thoughts that were beginning to build in his head.

On a shelf below the cashbox, Andrew found a pencil and paper. He returned to the confectionery shop.

Once again the children happily greeted him. They sat down in a circle and proceeded to recite the recipe. They quickly rattled off the ingredients necessary for the tarts. "Slow down," said Andrew. "I can't write that fast."

"How fast can you write?" asked Plumwell.

"As fast as I'm able to," said Andrew. And he

began to write *I write fast, I write fast, I write fast* on
a piece of paper.

"What does that say?" asked Peachum.

"It says *I write fast, I write fast, I write fast,*" said
Andrew.

"I'd like to be able to write fast," said Plumwell.

"I'd like to be able to write," said Prunella.

"It's really very easy," said Andrew. "Here, let
me show you how. Let us start from the beginning.
A, B, C—"

A dark shadow crossed over the shop. The children grew rigid with fright. Standing in the doorway was Celestial Grace, glowering with anger.

"What is going on here?" she yelled.

"Oh nothing," said Andrew, getting to his feet
and crumpling the piece of paper.

"What have you there?" she snarled.

Andrew put his hands behind his back.

"Give that to me," she said.

Andrew remembered Auntie Lizard's warnings
about Miss Celestial Grace, so he handed her the
piece of paper.

"A, B, C indeed!" she cried angrily.

The children shook; it was the worst case of the
shakes they had ever had.

Celestial Grace shredded the paper and screamed,
"Saboteur, get out!"

Andrew stuttered, "I-I-I w-w-was o-o-only t-t-try-
ing t-t-to—"

"Out!" she continued yelling. "And never come this way again!"

Andrew left the shop, frightened for himself and the children. He was also unhappy about not fulfilling his mission. "Now, how will I ever get Ashton the recipe for the ginger tarts?"

This time when he returned to the apothecary shop, Auntie Lizard was there. She was able to tell at once that something had gone wrong.

And when Andrew told her all the details, Auntie Lizard shook her head and said, "I hope we're not in for some really big trouble!"

17

Professor Effingham Humphries led Pooter through his grimy workshop. "Come, dog, you shall see my life's work, and set it in motion for me."

"I'd rather not see it," said Pooter. "I'm not interested in what you've been doing with your life. One thing is for sure, you haven't been too clean about it. This place smells worse than a hog barn on a hot day."

Pooter had no choice. He was taken to a large shrouded object.

"I shall make a fortune when I patent and sell this." The professor's eyes gleamed.

"What do I get out of it?" said Pooter wearily.

"You are now a witness to history," said the professor, removing the black cloth covering from the object. A broad grin crossed the professor's face, revealing an imperfect set of yellowing teeth. "This is my revolutionary treadmill. It churns butter and warms water for a footbath at the same time. And you, doggie, will make it happen."

"Too bad it doesn't brush teeth also—you sure could use it!" Pooter backed away from the treadmill. "I don't like your invention," he said. "I want no part of it!"

Pooter had no alternative. He was harnessed to the raked ramp of the treadmill, and to avoid sliding down he found himself having to run. "Oh, my poor legs!" he moaned.

"Wonderful, wonderful, brilliant!" shouted the professor, jumping up and down. The churn moved and vapors rose from the footbath. "My fortune is made."

"My legs are ruined," said Pooter.

Auntie Lizard paced about her shop nervously. She handed Andrew a feather duster and told him to clean the shelves.

"Save all the cobwebs," she said.

"Save the cobwebs?" questioned Andrew.

"Andrew, darling, their healing powers are incredible. Especially when used on swollen gums."

As Andrew dusted, he looked into the bottles and jars. They contained fragments of strange-looking matter that appeared to have been mined from a world beneath the ground. There were also molds and moss and knotted roots. Labels, water-stained and fading with age, had words written on them that seemed to come from a language that belonged to an ancient civilization. Andrew spoke the words softly, almost expecting something to happen after pronouncing each one. "Munadual, enneyac, bar-buhr."

Thunder rumbled and lightning flashed. Auntie Lizard uttered a cry. Andrew almost toppled from the stool he was standing on.

"What's the matter?" he said when he regained his footing.

"It's beginning to rain," said Auntie Lizard, looking out the shop window.

"Is that all?" said Andrew. And he returned to his dusting.

"Is that all!" whispered Auntie Lizard. "If it is Celestial Grace at work, it is enough!"

Farmer Van Aken finished the tree house, and when the girls saw it, they cried and said, "If only Andrew and Pooter were here to share it with us."

Mrs. Van Aken tried to cheer the girls up. She joined them in the tree house, bringing with her freshly made ice cream and sugar wafers.

"This is a special occasion," she said.

"It would be really special if everyone were here."

"When Andrew and Pooter return, we will have a real celebration," said Mrs. Van Aken.

"Do you think Pooter will ever come back?" The girls hugged their mother.

"Of course," said Mrs. Van Aken cheerily. "I've been praying for his safe return."

"So have we," said Meg.

"All the time," said Ellen.

"Good, then the Lord will answer our prayers," said Mrs. Van Aken.

"Do you think He's heard them?" asked Ellen.

Mrs. Van Aken looked at her daughters and smiled. "He hears so many prayers that sometimes it takes a while for Him to act on them."

"Do they sort of reach Him like letters?" asked Meg.

Mrs. Van Aken paused. "In a way," she said, thinking the question over herself.

After the children finished their ice cream and wafers, Mrs. Van Aken left the tree house and suggested that the girls decorate it.

Meg and Ellen responded enthusiastically to that idea. And they told themselves that the moment the Lord got their message, they were certain He would do something about it, because He knew how much Pooter meant to them.

Professor Effingham Humphries struggled with his treadmill as he tried to mount it on a wagon. Pooter watched helplessly in a cage.

"I hope it breaks into a million pieces," said Pooter.

The professor huffed, turned red in the face, and strained every muscle in his thin body as he pushed the treadmill onto the wagon.

When this chore was completed, he wiped his brow and wrung his hands. "Now for you!" he said, placing the caged Pooter on the wagon seat. "I can keep an eye on you here. Dogs have been known to get away, and you cost me a pretty penny."

"Where are we going?" asked Pooter.

"I bet you'd like to know where I'm taking you," said the professor. He got into the driver's seat and took hold of the reins. Then, with a birch-rod whip, he smacked the back of his horse. The horse was old, and his bony appearance told of his being underfed. Pooter could only feel sorry for him.

"Get going, horse!" shouted the professor.

At first the horse moved slowly, but the professor whipped him again, and the horse picked up his pace.

"We've got things to do!" cried the professor. "Money to be made, fame to be achieved."

"I still want to know where we are going," said Pooter.

They traveled a short distance, and once again Pooter found himself at the river's edge. Home is just across it, he told himself.

The air was sultry, Pooter warm and thirsty. The river looked refreshing.

"How about a swim?" said Pooter.

The professor left the wagon at the river's edge and walked to a grove of willow trees. They appeared to be floating on the water. The professor vanished amid their low, curtainlike branches. He reappeared walking along the riverbank with a large raft in tow.

Pooter's spirits were slightly cheered at the prospect of returning to the other side of the river. "If there were only a way to escape," he said.

The cage had bars of iron and a huge lock.

"It's hopeless," he said, and curled up, wanting to cry.

The professor led the horse and wagon onto the barge. Slowly they drifted across the river.

The cloudburst over Wiltwyck Landing continued. The narrow paths that went down to the river soon became gushing streams. As the rain continued the water level rose, and in some places front steps disappeared beneath it. Chickens atop baskets and kittens in crocks sailed by.

"If this continues," moaned Auntie Lizard, "my herbs will be part of an underwater garden."

Andrew noticed that the garden was rapidly becoming a pond. He was amazed to see such an enormous amount of rain fall in so short a time.

"Do sudden cloudbursts happen here often?" he asked.

"Only when you have a disgruntled neighbor," said Auntie Lizard, who was beginning to mop up some water that had started to seep into her kitchen.

Andrew raced for a mop when the water began to move into the shop. It all seemed futile, because after a while there wasn't anyplace to wring the mop out. The water began to rise quickly, and Jonas jumped to a high shelf. Auntie Lizard and Andrew sat on top of the counter.

Just when everything was about to float away, the rain stopped. The water receded slowly, and Auntie Lizard and Andrew went about cleaning up.

"It's a good thing the rain stopped when it did," said Andrew, "or we might all have been washed down to the river."

"Yes, one might say we were lucky this time," said Auntie Lizard, wringing out the hem of her dress.

At that moment the bell on the door jingled and Celestial Grace entered. "You look a bit soggy," she said, smiling.

Andrew hid when he saw who it was.

"Yes, I am a bit damp," said Auntie Lizard.

"One might say these sudden cloudbursts are but a warning!" Her eyebrow arched high to the top of her cap.

"A warning?" said Auntie Lizard.

"Yes, of things to come if some people continue their snooping pursuits. Look under every rain bar-

rel and all you'll find are worms and slugs. It's best to leave some things unturned. Do you agree?"

While she spoke Celestial Grace seemed to grow in size. At first Andrew thought his eyes were playing tricks on him, but when her head was but a few inches away from the ceiling he knew it wasn't his eyes. Jonas spit and ran behind some boxes.

Auntie Lizard held her ground and looked up at Miss Grace. "You're a big woman, Celestial, but there is the chance that one day you might get too big!"

Slowly Celestial Grace returned to her normal size. And when she was eye to eye with Auntie Lizard, she said, "In my business one can never be too big!"

"The bigger you are, the bigger your problems," said Auntie Lizard.

"I can handle all problems, just remember that!" said Celestial Grace, leaving the shop and slamming the door behind her. The bell jingled for moments afterward.

Andrew came out of his hiding place, trembling. "What's going on?" he asked. "Is that woman a magician?"

"Of sorts," answered Auntie Lizard briskly. "Come into the garden, Andrew. It's time for a talk."

18

Raindrops on the beech arbor were the only remainders of the sudden and fierce cloudburst. Auntie Lizard worked in the kitchen preparing lunch. Andrew wandered restlessly through the garden sniffing at the herbs and wondering what Auntie Lizard's talk would be about.

He was bewildered by her cheerful attitude when she entered the garden. It was as if nothing at all had happened. She placed a tray piled high with sandwiches on the table and motioned Andrew to join her.

Andrew sat next to Auntie Lizard. His nose tingled from smelling the herbs. The sandwiches looked good, but Andrew wasn't hungry. He was too preoccupied with the strange happenings, which he was beginning to find unsettling.

Auntie Lizard removed a fan from deep within her apron pocket and settled back in her chair, fanning herself. "Gardens are soothing retreats," she said, closing her eyes and breathing deeply.

Under different circumstances Andrew would

have agreed with her. But here in this garden the unexpected flourished.

Auntie Lizard helped herself to a sandwich. She had barely finished her first bite when she said, "Celestial Grace is a witch, and so am I!"

This revelation hit Andrew like a cold gust of wind. He felt every part of his body tremble.

"Don't be too alarmed, Andrew, dear. It's a fact that you'll just have to live with and adjust to. It's almost like saying summer is hot and winter is cold—you prepare for them and make the most of it. And no matter how much you might complain, it's not going to change things one way or another. So it is the case with witches. True? True!" Auntie Lizard asked and answered her own question.

Andrew just nodded in agreement, afraid to react otherwise.

"There are good witches and bad witches," she began again. "I'm a good one. Needless to say, Celestial Grace is a bad one. Although I must confess that the line is so thin, I find myself crossing over it every so often. What I might think is good is sometimes considered bad by others. It all gets so picky and choosey." She began to eat another sandwich. "If I do say so myself, these are delicious. Aren't you hungry, Andrew?"

"I-I sort of lost my appetite," said Andrew.

"Well, find it again. You'll need your strength.

You see, Celestial Grace is up to something big and terrible. I don't know what it is. I thought that perhaps you might find out something, some clue. That way we could fortify ourselves. Sometimes if we know in advance we can do something to counteract an awful happening. It's like treating an illness at the symptom stage.

"Jonas is my familiar," she said.

"Familiar?" asked Andrew.

"He helps me with my spells," said Auntie Lizard.

"Can't you work a spell against Celestial Grace, one that will make her good?" asked Andrew.

"An impossible task. I have acquired my craft as a witch. She is natural-born to it. Therefore I am helpless. Her power is stronger."

"That's too bad," said Andrew.

"Yes, it is!" agreed Auntie Lizard, shaking her head sadly.

"I feel sorry for the children she has adopted," said Andrew.

"Those poor dears. They would have been better off in the workhouse," said Auntie Lizard.

"Is there anything we can do to help them?" asked Andrew.

"We've tried," said Auntie Lizard. "The last attempt we made at rescuing those poor dears, the entire village almost went up in smoke."

"What happened?" asked Andrew, his curiosity aroused.

"All our chimneys got stuck. You can well imagine the mess. My eyes water and I have the urge to cough just thinking about it. I'm afraid we are just powerless against her." All traces of any cheerfulness had left Auntie Lizard. She appeared haggard.

"Perhaps I can help in some way," said Andrew, feeling very sorry for the children.

"No, no!" cried Auntie Lizard. "You have done enough already. If she catches you around there again, there's no telling what might happen."

The shop bell jingled. Auntie Lizard excused herself, and Andrew remained in the garden, thinking of ways he could rescue the children.

The raft drifted across the river as if pulled by an invisible rope. Evening colors appeared as it touched the far bank. Professor Humphries secured the raft and took the wagon ashore.

"Too bad I never got to join you, Andrew," said Pooter, looking wistfully across the river. "It looks as if I'll never see you again."

Clouds of amber, russet, and purple were reflected in the river. The wagon traveled the river road and then made a turn. The tannery came into sight. Pooter, who had his eyes on the kaleidoscopic river view, suddenly sat up as he realized he was traveling a familiar route. One that, if the professor kept to it, would lead to the tavern and little Sally.

A hopeful feeling took hold of Pooter and he almost felt like wagging his tail, something he hadn't done in a while.

The professor kept to the road. Just as things were turning to silhouettes the tavern came into view. Pooter had the almost uncontrollable urge to bark, but he didn't. All that he could hope for was that the wagon would stop there. I'm sure Sally will try to help me, he told himself.

The professor pulled the wagon up in front of the tavern. Little Sally appeared from within the tavern, barking and yelping. It was more than Pooter could stand. He returned her greeting.

"Quiet!" shouted the professor.

This command went unheeded. Pooter continued barking.

Mr. Tack joined Sally outside the tavern. "What's going on here?" he asked.

"I'm afraid this dog of mine is ill-mannered," said the professor. Once again he shouted for Pooter to keep quiet.

"Must be a dangerous dog if you keep it in a cage like that," said Mr. Tack.

"Oh, he's not dangerous," said the professor. "He's just eager. Eager to demonstrate this invention of mine." Professor Humphries made a broad sweeping gesture with his arm.

"Invention?" said Mr. Tack, nearing the wagon

and inspecting the treadmill. "What have you here?"

"My revolutionary treadmill. It churns butter and warms the water for a footbath at the same time." The professor got down from his wagon seat. "If you will be so kind and help me take it off the wagon, I will show you how it works."

Mr. Tack was curious. It wasn't every day that an inventor passed his way with a new machine. "We'd better take it into the tavern, where there is light," he said.

The two men groaned under the weight of the large treadmill. They set it down in the center of the tavern.

Sally remained outside and jumped up on the wagon seat. "Oh dear, Pooter, what's happened to you?" she asked.

"Everything," cried Pooter. "My trip has been disastrous."

Before they were able to exchange another word, the professor came out and took Pooter inside. He removed him from the cage and proceeded to harness him to the treadmill.

The diners in the tavern left their tables and gathered around the treadmill. Mr. Tack brought in fresh cream for the churn, and water for the footbath.

Pooter sighed. "I feel like a public spectacle," he said.

"Ladies and gentleman, you are about to see a preview of the twentieth century," announced the professor. And he set the treadmill in motion.

"OOOOpppss! Here goes," said Pooter, trying not to fall. He began to run, going nowhere.

"Poor Pooter!" cried Sally. "What trouble you are in!"

After a while Mr. Tack looked at the professor. "I don't see the churn turning." He felt the water in the tub. "This water doesn't seem to be warming up either."

"Just give it some time," said the professor nervously. "Great things don't happen quickly. Patience, patience."

Pooter felt his legs grow tired. He was tired and hungry. "Just because he's skinny and doesn't care about food," said Pooter, "it doesn't mean I shouldn't eat either. I'm hungry."

The professor kept yelling to Pooter, "Faster, faster!"

Pooter's mouth grew dry and his tongue hung out. "I can't go any faster," he said.

"Mr. Tack, make him stop, make him stop!" cried Sally, almost jumping to the tavern owner's ear.

Just as some vapor began to rise from the footbath, the treadmill went out of control. The churn and the footbath toppled over, covering the tavern floor with cream and water.

The diners jumped up on chairs, and Mr. Tack

grew red in the face. He shouted, "Get out! Get out! You and that damn fangled invention of yours. I should make you stay and clean this mess up, but just get out of my sight!"

Professor Effingham Humphries mopped his forehead and said, "Give it another chance, give it another chance!"

Mr. Tack continued to rage. "Take it away!" he commanded. "Take it away!"

The professor pulled and pushed at his treadmill, all the while slipping and sliding on the floor. Everyone laughed.

Pooter, who was still harnessed to the treadmill, couldn't help but laugh himself.

By the time the professor reached the front door he was coughing from exhaustion. Sally snapped at his heals.

"Dogs! I hate dogs!" he shouted. "It's all your fault!" he said, shaking his fist at Pooter.

"Don't blame me," said Pooter. "You've made your own trouble."

With every ounce of energy he could muster, the professor tried to mount the treadmill on the back of the wagon. The first few attempts were unsuccessful. When he did finally get it up on the edge of the wagon, the treadmill began to teeter back and forth. It swayed until it fell to the ground.

The horse neighed and pulled the wagon. Pooter felt his harness tear. When the jolt from having fallen passed, Pooter realized that he was free. The professor was sprawled on the ground under a heap of splinters and springs.

Pooter cried, "I'm free! I'm free!"

Sally came to his side. "I'm so happy for you," she said. "You'd better go now, before that mad-looking creature gets to his feet."

Pooter kissed Sally and ran off. The horse freed himself from the wagon and followed Pooter.

When Pooter saw what was happening, he said, "Come along. I'm sure the Van Akens will be happy to have you."

19

Andrew had arranged the bed so that if he lay on his stomach he was able to see out the small window. He was grateful for the starry night view, because he was unable to sleep. After a long while of star watching he felt as if he had become a part of the night.

Images of witches chasing him through the darkness filled his head. And when those thoughts faded, he replaced them with escape plans for the confectionery children. "If they could only hide someplace," he said. And then he wondered if it was possible to hide from a witch.

Andrew fell asleep as the first glow of dawn began to erase the stars. He was awakened by Auntie Lizard, who was standing over his bed.

"Are you all right?" she asked. "It's quite late, and since you weren't up, I grew worried and thought that perhaps the excitement of yesterday had made you ill. After all, the discovery of which witch is which can prove to be overwhelming, if not downright shocking!"

"I'm all right," yawned Andrew, and he rubbed his eyes.

"Good," said Auntie Lizard. "We have a busy day. You will have to make a delivery."

After breakfast Auntie Lizard handed Andrew some neatly tied packages. She told them they were to be delivered to the captain of the large sloop docked at Wiltwyck Landing pier.

"It's called the *Serpent's Eye*, and the captain's name is B. L. Zeebub. He's expecting you."

Andrew hurried down the winding street, and when he passed the confectionery shop he slowed his pace, hoping to catch a glimpse of the children and possibly get their attention.

Celestial Grace was at the window arranging some gingerbread, and when she saw Andrew her mouth turned down and her eyes became dark and angry. Andrew forced a smile. He tried to hide the fright he really felt.

The ship looked like a cauldron whose special cargo was secrets. It was long and black, with a serpentlike figurehead at the bow.

Andrew looked down at the parcels he was carrying and realized that he was delivering something that was sure to be used for some spell. He wanted to drop the packages and return to the other side of the river.

"Enough of Auntie Lizard," he told himself. Standing at the dock's edge, Andrew had thoughts only of home and wishing to be there.

These thoughts were shattered when a voice called out, "Looking for me, boy?"

Andrew looked up. Standing near the gangplank was an angular-looking man, with the blackest beard and eyebrows. His head was shaven so clean that the clouds were mirrored in it.

"I'm looking for B. L. Zeebub, the captain," said Andrew.

"Look no farther—I am he!"

Andrew walked up the gangplank. He felt the captain's eyes upon him and tried not to look up for fear of looking into them. Even at a distance, Andrew could tell they had a fierce animallike intensity about them.

"Eyes that can see in the darkness," Andrew told himself.

As Andrew neared the captain he smelled a familiar odor, but never had it been so strong before. It was the smell of rot in deep, unopened cellars. A smell so pungent that Andrew grew ill. He wanted to cover his nose and mouth and run. But as repellent as the smell was, there was something intoxicating about it. And Andrew breathed in deeper, almost wondering how much he could endure.

The test came to an abrupt end when the captain drew himself away from Andrew. "I understand you are Miss Hardwell's new assistant," he said.

It took a while before Andrew answered. "Yes sir, yes sir," he said.

"I shall be going up the river for a short run," said the captain, "but I shall be returning for the crescent moon party. Perhaps we can get to know each other better then."

Andrew nodded and said good-bye. As he left the ship, he was surprised to see Prunella and Plumwell about to board it. Their arms were laden with baskets.

"What are you doing here?" asked Andrew, surprised to see them.

"I was just about to ask you the same question," said Prunella.

"I was making a delivery, for Auntie Li— I mean I was delivering something," said Andrew.

"So are we," said Prunella.

"All these baked goods are for the ship," said Plumwell.

In a hushed voice Andrew said, "I'm glad I ran into you. I've got some very important information."

"You do?" they said, surprised.

"I'll wait here," said Andrew.

The children made their delivery and returned quickly. "What is it?" they asked eagerly.

Andrew stammered, "Th-th-th-this isn't going to be easy, but—but Miss Celestial Grace is a witch!"

"Of course she's a witch," said Prunella.

"An awful witch!" said Plumwell.

"You knew it all the time," said Andrew, almost disappointed.

"One just has to look at her to know that she's an awful witch," said Prunella.

Andrew shook his head. "No, I don't think you understand. She's a real witch, capable of terrible things. Spells, curses, and all things bad witches do!" The children looked both frightened and confused.

"We only joked around about her being a witch," said Prunella. "How did you get this information?"

"From Auntie Lizard—I mean Miss Hardwell. Remember that sudden storm yesterday, and the flooding? Well, it was Celestial Grace who arranged it."

"Oh, no!" cried Prunella. "What are we going to do? After last night we are going to be in real trouble—that is when she finds out!"

"Ssshh!" said Plumwell.

"Finds out what?" asked Andrew.

"After you left we decided that we were just determined to learn how to read." Prunella sighed. "We knew that Miss Grace had a private library in back of the supply room. Well, after she went to bed we sneaked in there and went through her books."

Plumwell held his nose. "They were the oldest and smelliest things you'd ever seen."

"When we touched them pages fell out, and bindings tore. We thought we heard Miss Grace stir so we hurriedly put things back. Only we didn't put them back in the right places. Nothing is in the right binding." Prunella wrung her hands. "Oh, boy! Are we in for trouble when she finds out!"

"What are we going to do?" said Plumwell.

Andrew looked toward the ship. "I just got an idea," he said. "This ship is leaving tonight for a trip up the river. Perhaps you can all sneak aboard and get away from her."

"She'll find us," said Prunella in tears.

"She will never find you in another place," said Andrew.

"We once wanted to talk to the minister, Uncle Hendrick. But she forbade it. She won't even allow us to go near the church," said Plumwell.

"That was the time we wanted to get away from her. Oh, it all makes sense now," said Prunella.

"What makes sense?" asked Andrew.

"So many things that all seemed so senseless before," answered Prunella.

Andrew looked around. "I feel uncomfortable talking here," he said, noticing that the captain was watching them.

"We don't have much time," said Plumwell.

"You are right in more ways than one," said Andrew.

Andrew led the children to a shady grove that bordered the village. There they sat down.

"Whenever we wanted to go to church, Miss Grace would have a fit," said Prunella. "I once heard that witches cannot and will not go into a church. They stay clear of anything that has to do with religion. It's just about the only thing that can do them in."

"Maybe if I went to the minister," said Andrew. "Oh no!" he said, remembering Peter Bronck and his mission.

"Oh no, what?" asked Plumwell.

"I just remembered that the minister isn't around," said Andrew. "I really think the only chance you have is to get aboard that ship and get away. Why don't you talk it over amongst yourselves? Then if you should decide to go, tonight when Miss Grace is asleep sneak out and come to the apothecary shop. I'll be waiting for you there. I will go with you to make sure everything is all right. The captain told me that he will be returning to Wiltwyck Landing. I'll just leave Auntie Lizard a note."

"Why are you spending the summer here?" asked Prunella.

"I think about that a great deal," said Andrew. "I have a feeling that it has to do with a promise my mother once made. Mothers sometimes do strange things," whispered Andrew.

"I wish I had a mother," said Plumwell.

At that moment Andrew found himself feeling

very sorry for the children. "I think it's best we aren't seen together anymore," he said. "Remember, I will be waiting for you tonight."

Auntie Lizard commented on Andrew's quiet behavior during dinner, and she asked him if there was anything wrong.

He assured her that things were fine.

"I realize how unsettling some discoveries can be," said Auntie Lizard. "But once you get used to them it's really quite easy to accept and live with them. Now that you know that I am a witch, it doesn't change your feelings toward me, does it, Andrew?" Auntie Lizard placed another helping of stew upon Andrew's plate.

Andrew was sorry she had done that. He had had trouble finishing his first helping. Bringing another forkful of stew to his mouth proved to be an impossible task. He placed his fork down and said, "I'm really quite full, thank you."

Auntie Lizard placed her own fork down and leaned over the table. She thrust her chin forward. "Is there something you are trying to conceal?" she asked in a low coaxing voice.

"No," said Andrew. "It's just too hot, and I'm not hungry."

"Too bad," said Auntie Lizard. "We'll have to forget about the strawberry sherbet dessert."

Auntie Lizard was surprised by Andrew's request to go to bed early.

When Andrew entered his small room he was sorry about his decision to retire early. Entering the room was like stepping into a foot warmer. The roof held the heat of the day, and the warm evening gave no indication of relief.

Andrew lost himself in his thoughts of the escape plan for the children. When he wasn't thinking about his plot, he listened. Listened to the familiar sounds of night in the house.

He heard Auntie Lizard turn the latch on the front door. And then the creak of the steps. The opening of her bedroom door and the shuffle of her feet across the room. He could even hear Jonas jump onto the bed with her.

Andrew listened and waited. When the sounds of sleep came from Auntie Lizard's room, he tiptoed down the stairs and made his way to the front of the shop. He proceeded carefully, so he wouldn't cause any disturbance. He lifted the door latch gently. A quiet sound came from behind Andrew, and his heart froze. At first he just wanted to run outside, but instead he looked over his shoulder. Sitting on the counter was Jonas.

"What are you doing here?" whispered Andrew. "Spying on me? I've got things to do. I'll be back; I've just got to help the children. They're in trouble." Andrew sighed. "And so am I!"

20

Pooter and the horse spent the day in hiding. They
hid in an overgrown orchard. It was the perfect
place to hide. It was cool and shady and offered
good protection.

"I think it will be safe to take to the open road
again in the morning," said Pooter. "And then I'll
take you to the Van Aken farm. Will they be surprised! I know they'll like you and you'll like them."

"I could sure use some love and tenderness," said
the horse. "And I can give it, too," he added.

"I'm sure of that," said Pooter. He was happy to
be of help to the horse. Just looking at him, one
could tell that he had been mistreated.

"Do you think the professor has given up hunting
for us?" asked the horse.

"I'm certain he has, but we'll just stay in hiding
a little longer to make sure," said Pooter.

"Professor Humphries really isn't a very nice person," said the horse.

Pooter agreed with him. "Wait until you meet
Andrew," he said.

"Who is Andrew?" asked the horse.

"He is my best friend," said Pooter. "He is away from the farm, so you won't be meeting him right away. But when he does return, I know you'll take to each other."

"Can I be your best friend also?" asked the horse.

"You already are," said Pooter.

Andrew closed the shop door behind him and stepped outside. A river mist rolled through the village hiding whatever the darkness of night didn't. Frightened, Andrew pressed his back against the shop door.

He lifted the latch, wanting to go back inside, but the door didn't open. Andrew felt panicky and he wanted to yell. But he kept quiet, and told himself that the children would be along any minute.

He listened for their sound, and when he did hear footsteps, he whispered, "It's me, Andrew. I'm here."

The footsteps got closer, and when the sound was almost upon him Andrew was able to see the shape of a head. Inches away he saw the face of the charred beggar. Andrew wanted to run, but he was trapped between the beggar and the shop door.

He felt the beggar's hand take hold of his. "Come with me," said the raspy-voiced old man. "The children are waiting for you."

Andrew tried to free himself from the beggar's

strong grip, but he was unable to do so. "Don't be afraid," said the beggar. "I'm just helping the children out. They are expecting you, are they not?"

The old beggar walked quickly. A pace that belonged to a younger person, thought Andrew, who had difficulty keeping up with him. In order to avoid being dragged, Andrew quickened his step, which was almost a run.

Andrew couldn't help but be astonished at how well the old man made his way through the dark night.

Visions of the old beggar at the tavern, and then at the pier, flashed before Andrew's eyes. Who is this strange old creature? he asked himself. Is he really taking me to the children?

Andrew's questions were soon answered. He found himself ushered into a room where the children were all huddled together, crying.

Right before their eyes the beggar shook and pulled at himself and became Miss Celestial Grace.

The children stopped crying as they watched this magical transformation.

"Surprise!" shouted Celestial Grace. "So you thought you could plot against me, foolish, foolish children! Don't you know I have eyes in the back of my head?"

Celestial Grace turned her back and lifted up her cap and curls, revealing a set of eyes on the back of her head.

The children trembled.

"Tremble my darlings, tremble! If you knew what I have in store for you, you'd really be sick." She laughed and left the room, locking it.

"It's all my fault," said Andrew.

"Don't blame yourself," said Prunella. "You only meant well."

"I suppose it had to happen sooner or later," said Pearetta, her eyes red from crying.

"What do you think she is going to do to us?" asked Plumwell.

Andrew shrugged. "With her power," he said, "I'd rather not think about it."

The children began to cry again.

Celestial Grace returned with a big leather book under her arm and lots of little cloth sacks in her hands.

"You'll pay for your treachery," she said.

"That's one of the books we messed up," whispered Prunella.

"Whispering behind my back, that won't help your situation," said Celestial Grace.

She drew a circle on the floor and ordered the children into it. She kept referring to the book, and removed things from the little sacks and placed them near the circle. The outer rim of the circle was soon decorated with bones, roots, and strange-looking minerals.

Celestial Grace began to shout. "By the time I'm

through with you, you'll all be squealing puppies!"
She danced around the circle waving a wand with a
long hairy tail at its tip. Then she said, "Sgod, sgod,
nrut ot sgod!"

Celestial Grace did this a few times. The children
held each other tightly. Andrew said, "Oh, Lord,
please help us!"

Celestial Grace continued her dance and then she
screamed out as if in pain. The children watched in
wonder as she began to shrink and squeal. A long
hairless tail grew from her back, and her face became pointed and furry. Her eyes were reduced to
little black beads. Miss Celestial Grace turned into
a rat.

The children shrieked with delight and clapped
their hands. The rat ran frantically for cover.

"Her spell worked against her," said Andrew.

"It must have been the mix-up of the pages and
their coverings," said Prunella.

"I was praying awfully hard," said Andrew.
"Maybe it was the prayer."

"Maybe both!" said Plumwell.

"Whatever," said Peachum, "it worked!"

The children chased the squealing rat around the
room.

"Let's get it!" said Appleton.

"Be careful," said Andrew. "Rats bite!"

"I'll get a trap," said Plumwell. Running to get
one, he opened the door.

"Watch out!" shouted Andrew. "It will escape!"

Andrew's warning was too late; the rat made its way out of the storeroom.

The children began to chase it through the shop and up into the house, some shouting, "Get that rat!"

And others, "Get Miss Grace!"

Andrew shouted, "Get that Celestial rat!"

Upstairs, downstairs, in cupboards, out of cupboards, the children kept up the chase. Several times the rat squealed loudly and showed its large curved teeth. When that happened the children backed away.

The rat made its way to the bedroom, under the bed, and out the window.

"We've lost it!" the children shouted, racing downstairs. They ran outside, hoping to find the rat again.

There in front of the shop was the rat catcher holding a squealing Celestial rat by the tail.

"Journey's end," he said, placing the squirming rat in one of the many little cages that hung from a long pole.

The children applauded the rat catcher, who took a deep bow. "I'm only doing my job," he said.

"But that's a very special rat you've got there," said Andrew.

"Special?" said the rat catcher, looking closely at his newest catch. "All rats look the same to me."

The river mist had pulled away, uncovering a bright new morning. The children waved happily as they watched the rat catcher wend his way to the river.

"This is cause for celebration," said Prunella.

The children went into the shop, and they began to stuff themselves with their own goodies.

"I must say I'm a very good baker," said Plumwell, biting deep into a custard eclair.

"So am I," said Appleton, eating a chocolate-chip cookie.

Andrew sampled everything, and said he was too stuffed to walk.

As the morning light grew brighter and moved into the shop, Andrew said, "I'd better return to Auntie Lizard, or she will worry. I didn't leave a note behind."

"What's to become of us?" asked Appleton.

"I'll tell Auntie Lizard about everything that's happened. Perhaps she will be able to help us," said Andrew.

"In the meantime we will open the shop and continue as if nothing had happened," said Prunella.

"Good idea," said Andrew. "See you later."

Andrew returned to the shop. There he found Auntie Lizard pacing about and rapidly fanning herself. When she saw Andrew, she sank into a chair and cried, "Where have you been, child? I am at the very edge of insanity. Your disappearance caused me great anguish. I was just about to seek the services of Simon the Seer." Putting her hands to her hips and, wrinkling up her mouth, Auntie Lizard said, "Now give me your explanation—and it had better be a good one!"

Auntie Lizard listened as Andrew unfolded his tale of the night's happenings. He was repeatedly interrupted by ohs and ahs from Auntie Lizard.

And when he came to the part of how Miss Grace was transformed into a rat, Auntie Lizard shrieked with joy and kissed Andrew.

Then she took his hands and danced around the shop and into the garden. It ended when Auntie Lizard collapsed, laughing. "Water, water!" she cried, sitting in a patch of marjoram.

The closest available water was in the watering can, which Andrew immediately sprinkled on Auntie Lizard.

Andrew and Auntie Lizard were taken by surprise.

Ashton Dansforth was standing at the entranceway to the garden. "Well!" he said, folding his hands across his chest.

"Oh, Ashton, you wouldn't believe what has happened," said Auntie Lizard. Andrew helped her to her feet.

"If the scene I have just witnessed is any indication of what you are going to tell me, I must say I'm prepared for anything!"

"Ashton darling, are you prepared for the demise of Miss Celestial Grace?" cooed Auntie Lizard.

Ashton slumped to the ground in a faint.

21

Meg and Ellen were in the tree house making a bed of leaves for their dolls. "Sleep, sleep, little dolly. The leaves are cool," said Ellen. "Put your dolly to sleep."

Meg said, "My dolly doesn't want to sleep; she wants to stay awake and look at the treetops."

Meg held her doll high. "Look, pretty dolly. Look at the trees, and the sky." Meg grew silent, her eyes widened, and she put down her doll. "Look! Look!" she cried. "It's Pooter, with a horse!"

Ellen ran to her sister's side. "Pooter! Pooter!" she cried.

Pooter made his way to the barn, with the horse close behind.

The children raced down from the tree house and ran to Pooter, crying and laughing.

"What a reception!" Pooter said. He barked loudly as the girls hugged and kissed him. "See, I told you they loved me here."

The horse whinnied.

"Where have you been?" they asked. "We were so worried."

"We missed you so much," said Ellen, wiping her eyes on Pooter's ears.

"And who are you?" asked Meg, gently stroking the horse.

"He's a friend of mine," said Pooter. "In much need of love and understanding."

Farmer and Mrs. Van Aken came running from the barn when they heard the noisy return.

Mrs. Van Aken wiped her eyes with her apron hem. "Welcome home, Pooter," she sobbed.

Farmer Van Aken got to his knees and gave Pooter a good petting. "Pooter, where did you find this horse?" he asked. "Whoever your friend is, he is in need of attention. He has been badly cared for."

"You can say that again," said Pooter.

"And where did you go off to?" asked the farmer.

"If I ever told you what I've been through," said Pooter, "you wouldn't believe me. I'll try to forget it. I wish Andrew were here to greet me."

"Too bad Andrew isn't here," said Mrs. Van Aken.

"He will be here at summer's end," said Farmer Van Aken, sounding as if he were trying to convince his family as well as himself about his son's return.

"When that happens we'll really celebrate," said Pooter.

Farmer Van Aken took the horse into the barn

and fed him a good meal. Then the girls brushed him.

"I knew they would like you," said Pooter.

The horse thanked Pooter and told him that this was the happiest he'd ever been.

Pooter feasted also. The children said, "Please, Pooter, don't ever leave us again."

"You don't have to worry about that," said Pooter, and he found a nice cool spot and went to sleep.

Ashton recovered and listened joyfully to the details of Andrew's story.

"Celestial Grace thought she would render us all powerless by taking away our reading and writing abilities." Auntie Lizard put her hands to her face. "I shudder to think of what would have happened if she had succeeded."

"Andrew, I think you're going to have a promising career," said Ashton, winking to Auntie Lizard. "Don't you think so, Auntie dear?"

"But of course," said Auntie Lizard, her head nodding in agreement.

"What about the children?" asked Andrew. "What's going to happen to them?"

"We will think of something," said Auntie Lizard. "For the present I'm sure they can care for themselves."

"Right now we have to think about the crescent moon celebration," said Ashton. "It is tonight, and I have your costume."

"You do?" said Andrew. "Can I see it?"

"In a little while," said Ashton.

The shop bell rang, and Auntie Lizard asked Andrew to go and see who it was, and if they needed any help to take care of them. "I think you are quite capable of handling things," said Auntie Lizard proudly.

Andrew went into the shop.

Ashton looked at Auntie Lizard. "Does he know about us?" he asked.

"Yes, I told him," said Auntie Lizard.

"Does he know that he will soon be joining our ranks?"

Auntie Lizard didn't answer right away. She walked along a garden path and stopped to pick some weeds. "No, I didn't tell him that he would soon be one of us. After all, he is a child, and there is a limit to what he can comprehend. Hearing about someone else's peculiar abilities is one thing, but learning about oneself is another matter."

Ashton cried, "Do you have something on the stove?"

"No," answered Auntie Lizard, turning her eyes to the kitchen.

Clouds of smoke came drifting into the garden.

"I should have known better," said Auntie Lizard solemnly. "It's Celestial Grace!"

Andrew came running into the garden, coughing, his eyes watery. "What's happening?" Ashton asked.

He looked toward the chimney. A bird chattered nervously above it.

"A bird has chosen the chimney for a nesting place." Andrew pointed upward.

"A poor choice of places," said Ashton.

"For all concerned," said Auntie Lizard, getting lost in the clouds of smoke that settled around her.

Andrew got a ladder and made his way up it. He told the bird not to be afraid.

With great care, Andrew gently removed the nest from the chimney and placed it in the beech arbor. The bird flew away and Andrew felt as if his entire work had been in vain.

After the smoke cleared, Ashton suggested that they repeat their first garden meal. Everyone was in agreement. And as before it was Andrew's chore to get the dessert.

The children were happy to see Andrew so soon again. They told him that all was well at the shop.

"And not a rodent in sight," said Plumwell.

Prunella told Andrew that she was eagerly awaiting the minister's return so that they could begin their lessons in reading.

"And writing," said Appleton, who was sprawled on the shop floor drawing pictures.

Andrew returned to the garden and Ashton's river-fish lunch. Chunks of fish swam in a creamy sauce. "My very own recipe," said Ashton, acknowledging the compliments given to him by Andrew and Auntie Lizard.

After the very last crumb of dessert had disappeared, Ashton leaned back in his chair and thrust his head backward. "Now that the air has cleared, I can easily predict that tonight will be a clear one for the summer's crescent moon.

A growing curiosity about his costume and what the party would be like began to consume Andrew. He grew visibly restless. Restless to a point that Auntie Lizard asked him if he was feeling well.

"I think it's time!" said Ashton, jumping to his feet.

"Time for what?" asked Andrew eagerly.

"Time for me to paint your portrait," said Ashton.

"My portrait?" said Andrew, startled by Ashton's announcement.

"Andrew, you have a most interesting face. And not only that, you are something of a hero, and heroes must be painted."

"But I'm not a hero," said Andrew.

"Savior, hero, why quibble with words? Call yourself what you will. Nevertheless, dear boy, your deed has set you apart from the ordinary. You were instrumental in the removal of Celestial Grace."

"But it was something she brought upon herself," said Andrew in protest.

Auntie Lizard fluttered her hands. "Nonsense! Directly or indirectly, you did bring about the fall of a terrible being. Which will add immeasurably to the festivities of tonight!" Auntie Lizard got up, lifted the hem of her skirt, and curtsied to Andrew.

Andrew felt his face redden, and he wanted to crawl under the table.

"All that modest blushing will soon come to an end," said Ashton. And he went inside the house. "Dear Andrew, if you only knew the importance of the occasion," he whispered to himself.

Auntie Lizard danced around the table clapping her hands over her head. "Tonight's the night for celebration!" she sang.

"What exactly is going to happen?" asked Andrew.

"Surprise! Surprise! Why ruin something wonderful by knowing in advance what to expect?"

Surprise, fine, thought Andrew, but I would like a hint.

Auntie Lizard flopped into her chair and sighed deeply. "I just really can't believe it yet," she said. "But something has been accomplished that people have tried for years to do. Why, do you know that the removal of Celestial Grace is almost akin to rid-

ding the world of the plague? And you know what a truly monumental feat that is!" Auntie Lizard shook her head. "It's so easy to believe terrible things; why is it so difficult to truly believe something wonderful?"

Auntie Lizard looked at Andrew, almost expecting an answer.

Andrew's response was just a shrug of his shoulders.

The bird returned to his nest, and Andrew was happy to see that his effort had proved to be worthwhile.

Ashton practically flew into the garden carrying his large folio with papers. And wearing his hat with the brushes tucked into the hatband.

"Are we ready?" he asked.

Andrew wasn't too sure what he had to do in order to get ready for the portrait-painting session.

Sounding very much like a doting mother, Auntie Lizard said, "Ashton is really an extraordinary painter."

Ashton seated himself opposite Andrew. And using his large folio as a lap table, Ashton began to draw Andrew.

Andrew found himself growing very self-conscious, which prompted Ashton to say, "Be natural—don't stiffen up. We just want the sweet natural you for all posterity."

Andrew then wondered if the painting would still

be around when he was an old man, and perhaps after his death. His thoughts then turned to heaven and hell, and deep down he had a feeling that he was a part of something that was in defiance of everything he had been taught in Sunday school. And that perhaps there wouldn't be a place for him in paradise when he left this mortal world. As he dwelled on the subject he grew uncomfortable—so much so that Ashton asked him what was wrong.

It took a remark from Auntie Lizard to take him from his thoughts. "Andrew, remove that cloud from your face. Do you want to be remembered as an unhappy young man?"

Andrew forced a smile.

"Better, better, better," said Ashton.

Ashton became the object of Andrew's attention, and suddenly Andrew began to laugh. He thought Ashton looked really silly with his brush-holder hat.

"What's so funny?" asked Ashton. "Is it my hat?"

Andrew nodded his head yes.

Ashton smiled wryly. "Just wait until you see your portrait!"

"Will I be able to show it to my family?" asked Andrew.

Auntie Lizard came around to Andrew and placed her hand on his shoulder. "In time," she said. "In time . . ."

22

The looking glass reflected a strange, unfamiliar creature as Andrew stood in front of it. Auntie Lizard and Ashton stood by, beaming proudly. "What a remarkable transformation!" they said.

Andrew looked at himself from under the skins of an old goat, and an odorous one at that. He was warm and uncomfortable under the weight of the costume, and it was an effort for him not to hold his nose.

"You'll have a marvelous time, I promise you that!" said Auntie Lizard, dressed in a black, long flowing cloak.

Andrew couldn't imagine himself having a marvelous time, looking or feeling as he did.

Ashton was dressed in a bottle-green cloak that had a hood. "Don't admire yourself too long," said Ashton. "We must be leaving soon."

Before they left the shop Auntie Lizard gave them torches, and once outside they lighted them.

They walked toward the river and were soon joined by others in similar dress, carrying torches also. When they reached the river the group took on a processionlike appearance.

A crescent moon hung low over the river. Its reflection created the image of large script letter E. E for evil, thought Andrew.

The silent procession was soon broken by whispering. The whispering became a low steady noise, and that became a chant.

Sthginot eht thgin
fo eht tnecserc noom,
a emitremmus cilorf
rof yreve nool.

The torch-carrying parade walked along the river-bank, and when the marchers passed the small wall-enclosed cemetery they joined hands and danced around it. Andrew was glad he was sandwiched between Auntie Lizard and Ashton—they showed him what to do.

After they danced around the cemetery a few times, they continued their walk along the river. The walk ended at a rocky cove.

Andrew watched, startled, as the procession disappeared into a cave in the cove. Frightened, Andrew balked at entering the cave. Auntie Lizard had to give him a nudge from behind. Andrew moved reluctantly ahead.

Once inside, the procession wove its way through a long tunnel. At the tunnel's end they were outside again at what appeared to be another river. The crescent moon loomed larger than it had before, and the large reflected E seemed to be suspended.

A dark shape appeared from the center of the E. As the shape neared, Andrew was able to see that it was the black ship of B. L. Zeebub.

The ship's landing and his appearance at the helm caused great jubilation. Andrew felt left out not responding more enthusiastically, but he did tell himself that he had only seen the man once before, and that everyone else must be an old friend of his.

At a given signal from the ship's captain, everyone removed his cloak. Andrew was surrounded by pigs, sheep, cows, crows, chickens, and goats like himself. Auntie Lizard was dressed as a chicken, and Ashton was a sheep.

A pig wove through the crowd carrying a large trough, from which everyone drank.

When it was offered to Andrew he wanted to refuse it, but once again he felt Auntie Lizard's hand behind him, nudging him to drink.

It looked very much like the color of blood, and Andrew closed his eyes when he drank. To his surprise, the liquid had a sweet cherry flavor, and he drank lots.

The drink left Andrew with a giddy feeling, and he covered his mouth because he wanted to laugh. It didn't matter, because soon everyone was laughing.

B. L. Zeebub played on a flute. And everyone

began to dance to the lively tune he was playing. Andrew danced with Auntie Lizard and Ashton.

As the music grew more spirited and the dancing livelier, those dressed as pigs began to oink, those as cows to moo, and everyone made noises according to his respective costume.

Andrew bleated.

The louder he bleated the quieter the others got, and soon Andrew was the focus of all attention. A circle gathered around him.

B. L. Zeebub stopped his flute playing and went to Andrew's side, carrying a large flask containing an amber-colored oil. He poured the oil over Andrew and everyone shouted at once.

Andrew turned around, shaking the oil from himself.

While he did this, Captain B. L. Zeebub, said,

*"I ma eht gnik fo ssenkrad
dna uoy llahs eb a ylecnirp kcolraw."*

After these words were said everyone jumped up and down shouting, "B. L. Zeebub, B. L. Zeebub, B. L. Zeebub!"

As Andrew continued spinning, the crowd, crescent-moon sky, and river became one. He was lifted high in the air and passed from shoulder to shoulder. When it was Ashton's turn he said, "Having a good time, Andrew?"

Andrew dizzily nodded his head yes.

The whirling frenzy gradually faded, with everyone collapsing to his knees.

The ship's crew, a band of winged gnomes carrying long forklike implements, marched around singing,

> "Laitselec ecarg
> sah neeb tup ot tser,
> werdna nav neka
> sah dessap sih tset!"

Andrew sat cross-legged in a circle, and candles
were placed around him. One by one, they came
and lighted them.

"It's like a giant birthday, only without the cake,"
said Andrew. Those were his last words that night.
The goat skin had grown very heavy, and the smoke
made Andrew's eyes burn. He closed them.

The bird in the beech arbor called, and Andrew
rolled over in bed. He rubbed his eyes and thought
he had just left a dream behind.

The smell of the goat skin was still with him, and
Andrew woke up knowing that the night had been
a real experience.

Auntie Lizard knocked on the door and entered
the room, smiling. "Sleepyhead, it's afternoon," she
said.

Andrew raised himself on his elbows. "I must have been really tired."

"It *was* a big night—your night, Andrew!"

"My night?" Andrew looked at Auntie Lizard quizzically.

"You were guest of honor!" she said, somewhat taken aback that Andrew hadn't been aware of his privilege.

Auntie Lizard left the room, and Andrew got out of bed and dressed. A light-headedness came over him as he walked down the stairs to the shop. He shook his head, hoping to rid himself of it.

"A good meal and you'll feel fine," said Auntie Lizard, who had been observing him.

The meal Auntie Lizard had prepared was a good one, and Andrew ate heartily. When he asked where Ashton was, Auntie Lizard told Andrew that Ashton had left. "He had important things to do," she said. "He left something behind for you."

Auntie Lizard went into the shop and returned moments later carrying an artist's board. She turned it around, and Andrew was happily surprised to see a completed painting of himself. He thought the likeness was a good one, and said, "Ashton is really talented!"

"You are a handsome devil," smiled Auntie Lizard.

Andrew had seconds, and after he had finished them she asked, "How do you feel now?"

Andrew said he felt just fine.

"Good," cooed Auntie Lizard. "I did hope last night's experience wouldn't leave you with any ill aftereffects. Well," she said casually, "you are one of us now."

"One of what?" cried Andrew, jumping up from the table.

His cry was so loud that Jonas ran up on a shelf and hid in a crock.

"Don't be excited. Now see what you've done. Come here, Jonas," said Auntie Lizard waving her arm.

"What is it that I am?" asked Andrew. His voice trembled.

"You, dear boy, can now proudly call yourself a warlock." Auntie Lizard began to clear the table.

"A warlock!" cried Andrew. "I don't want to be a warlock," he said.

"Andrew, sometimes we don't have choices. Anyway, there are a lot worse things you could be. I'm glad Ashton isn't here; he would be terribly insulted."

Jonas poked his head out of the crock and jumped down from the shelf. He went up to Andrew and rubbed himself against his leg, purring.

"See?" said Auntie Lizard. "Jonas loves you."

Andrew buried his face in his hands and wanted to cry, but no tears fell.

23

Peter Bronck and the minister, Uncle Hendrick, waited for the ferry to arrive. "Another job well done," said the minister, placing his hand on Peter's shoulder. Peter smiled proudly.

"I wonder what has gone on in my absence," said the minister.

"We'll soon know," said Peter.

Uncle Hendrick rubbed his hand through his hair. "I can't help but think my being called away was part of a scheme."

The ferryboat arrived and Mr. Gaty greeted them warmly. "Did everything get taken care of?" he asked.

"Yes." Uncle Hendrick sighed.

"What was it this time?" Mr. Gaty asked.

"Some parents were behaving badly. They were mistreating their children. All is fine now."

"Good," said Mr. Gaty.

"Now it is my turn to ask a question of you," said the old minister. "What has been happening in my absence?"

"The strangest thing is the disappearance of Miss Celestial Grace," said Mr. Gaty.

"Celestial Grace gone!" said the minister, startled.

"I know it's hard to believe, but she just isn't around."

"Are you sure she isn't up to something?" said the minister.

"We asked the children, and they said she will never return. They have been telling everyone that she is dead."

"Dead!" The minister repeated the word as if he had never heard it before. "I wonder how it happened. Could have been B. L. Zeebub that did her in. She was getting too big for her britches."

"The children have been pretty closemouthed about how it happened. But they are eager to see you."

"And I them." The minister wiped his face with his handkerchief and then blew his nose. He raised his eyes upward. "Is it really possible that Celestial Grace is dead?"

Rays of golden light fell upon the river. "It certainly is a lovely day," said the minister. "Peter, have you your friend's book?"

"Right here," said Peter. "It's never left my side. I'll be returning it first thing."

"I can't cry," said Andrew.

"That's one of the advantages of being a warlock," chirped Auntie Lizard.

"Advantages?" said Andrew.

"Too numerous to count," said Auntie Lizard.

Auntie Lizard beckoned Andrew to follow her into the shop. This was a signal for Jonas, who went along also.

"With a brand-new facet to your being, you also have talents that you never dreamed of." Auntie Lizard disappeared beneath the counter and burrowed molelike among the large volumes she had stored there.

She whispered to herself, "J—K—L, oh yes, we'll start out with something really marvelous."

Andrew grew anxious as Auntie Lizard prattled on. "Oh Andrew, with your green eyes and left-handedness you'll be a natural, like a bat at night."

"What does the color of my eyes and my being left-handed have to do with anything?" asked Andrew.

"A lot!" said Auntie Lizard. "It makes things much easier when working spells."

"I don't want to work any spells. What will my family say?"

"Family? Family? I am your family," said Auntie Lizard with a touch of hurt to her voice. She put down the large book she was holding. "Now, where were we before this family talk began?"

"We were at the letter L," said Andrew.

"Why yes, yes of course. L, L for levitation," said Auntie Lizard, opening the book.

"Levitation?" Andrew appeared dumbfounded.

"Yes, the art of raising things off the ground." Auntie Lizard scanned the page. Pushing her face close to the book, she mumbled to herself. And then went running around the shop gathering things off the shelves. Dust flew, making her cough and sneeze. "Haven't levitated anything for years."

In a short time there was an assortment of boxes, bottles, and jars assembled on the counter top.

"Come here, Andrew." Auntie Lizard called him to her side. "This is going to be your spell!"

Andrew was suddenly excited. It was almost the same feeling he would get before swinging from the high hayloft. Excited and frightened at the same time.

"Don't be afraid, dear," said Auntie Lizard. "You have the power; now all you need is the recipe and the proper ingredients, and here they are!" She moved her arm over the counter with a broad sweeping gesture.

In one jar Andrew noticed tadpoles swimming backward. "How odd," he said.

"Upward-moving water gathered downward. A very important ingredient, I might add."

"What is this?" asked Andrew, picking up a twisted piece of wood.

"Root from now the now-extinct lumell tree, a very rare item indeed." Auntie Lizard looked at the root wistfully. "In time to come there will be fewer

spells for us to work. So many things necessary for
true magic are becoming extinct. One of your func-
tions as a warlock is also to preserve. In my lifetime
I have seen many wonderful things vanish. Be a
guardian, Andrew; there's great magic in nature. . . ." Auntie Lizard's voice trailed off.

Jonas seated himself on the counter near Andrew.

"Are you going to watch me work my spell?"
Andrew asked Jonas.

"He is going to help you," said Auntie Lizard.
"You can borrow Jonas' services for this spell, but
for the future you'll have to acquire your own familiar."

"Pooter will become my familiar," said Andrew.

"Dogs don't make good familiars," said Auntie
Lizard.

"Why?" asked Andrew.

"Oh, dogs are too—too down-to-earth. Cats are a
bit more otherworldy."

"I don't know any cats," said Andrew.

"Jonas will introduce you to some. Won't you,
dear?" Auntie Lizard caressed the cat until he
purred loudly. "You're going to assist Andrew. It's
the levitation spell. Mmm—what shall we raise off
the ground?"

Auntie Lizard wandered around the shop trying
to decide upon what object Andrew would levitate.
While she was doing that, Andrew became deeply
engrossed in the book. So much so that he began to

follow the directions. He put everything in place and said, "Are you ready, Jonas?" Then he rolled up his sleeves and began to chant.

> *"Tel eht nosrep taolf hgih ni eht ria*
> *tel mih taolf tuohtiw a erac!"*

Suddenly Auntie Lizard was lifted off her feet. She began to giggle. "Oh Andrew, what have you done?"

"It works! It works!" he shouted excitedly.

Auntie Lizard floated through the shop and into the garden.

"I'm a real warlock!" Andrew picked Jonas up and kissed him. "We've made magic! We've made magic!"

Auntie Lizard giggled, floating upside down under the beech arbor.

The shop bell rang and Peter Bronck came in.

His unexpected arrival took Andrew by surprise. "Peter!" he exclaimed. "It's—it's good to see you."

"Good to see you, Andrew," he said. Peter looked at the counter with all its spell-creating ingredients. "What are you up to?" he asked.

"Oh—I'm—I'm taking inventory," stammered Andrew.

"You seem different," said Peter. He wrinkled his nose and sniffed. "You also smell different."

"I do?" said Andrew, bringing his forearm up to

his nose. "I suppose it's hard to smell oneself." He took a deep breath and his nose was filled with a dank cellarlike smell. "I'd better bathe," he said.

"I have something for you," said Peter.

"Something for me?" said Andrew, surprised.

"Yes, it was left behind on the ferry by a dog." A puzzled expression crossed Andrew's face. Peter handed Andrew his prayer book.

"My prayer book!" said Andrew, startled.

A loud thud and cry came from the garden. Auntie Lizard came into the shop, brushing herself off. "What's going on here?" she asked crossly when she saw Peter Bronck.

Andrew held up the book. "It's just Peter returning my prayer book!" he said.

"*Prayer book!*" screamed Auntie Lizard. "It's all ruined now!"

"What's ruined?" said Andrew.

"Everything! He's ruined everything. You can return home now," said Auntie Lizard. She covered her eyes with one hand and pointed with the other. "That book, that book did you in!"

"It's only my prayer book," said Andrew, walking toward Auntie Lizard with it.

"Only your prayer book! Stay where you are!" she shrieked.

Peter Bronck laughed. "The weapon against witchcraft," he said.

Auntie Lizard went into the garden.

Andrew was happy to see Peter Bronck again, and he was eager to see his family. But he was a little disappointed about not being able to work any more spells. It did seem like fun.

Andrew packed his things and went into the garden to say good-bye to Auntie Lizard. She was slumped in a chair wearing an expression of deepest gloom.

"I just want to say good-bye and thank you for everything," he said.

She raised her drooping eyelids and looked at Andrew. "Too bad things didn't work out. You had great potential. Have a safe trip, Andrew."

Andrew walked through the shop and a sadness came over him. A tear fell. "I can cry again," he said to Jonas, and rubbed the cat good-bye.

Peter Bronck was waiting outside the shop for Andrew. "We'll go home together," he said. "My eldest brother will be waiting on the other side of the river."

As they approached the confectionery shop, Andrew said, "I have to say good-bye to some friends."

The children were excited. They greeted Andrew, all speaking at once. Prunella told them to hush up. She then told Andrew that the minister, Uncle Hendrick, had come by and said that he would look after them.

"He's going to teach us how to read," said Plumwell.

"And write too!" said Appleton.

"We might write our very own cookbook," said Prunella.

Andrew told the children he was leaving, and that if they ever journeyed across the river they should come by and visit him.

The children all hugged Andrew good-bye, and Prunella kissed him.

Andrew felt himself grow red. Peter Bronck laughed.

At the river's edge Andrew saw a rat dart under the dock. He thought it looked like the Celestial Grace rat. But then he told himself that all rats look alike. Or do they?

24

Peter Bronck's brother was waiting on the other side of the river, just as Peter had said. All the way home Andrew kept thinking about his prayer book and its mysterious appearance on the ferry. He wondered if the dog involved had been Pooter. The more he thought about the book and Pooter, the more unanswered questions began to fill his head. He also began to wonder if Pooter would be at the farm to greet him on his return.

When the wagon came in sight of the big elm tree that marked the beginning of the farm, Andrew had his answer. Pooter greeted him with the loudest barking he had ever heard.

Andrew jumped down from the wagon and hugged and kissed Pooter hello. He thanked Peter and his brother and told them to come by soon. Peter said he would.

Pooter's noisy greeting brought the entire Van Aken family out to greet Andrew. They all laughed and cried. And Meg and Ellen couldn't wait to tell Andrew about the new horse that Pooter had found, and show him the tree house.

"Auntie Li—Elizabeth felt perfectly well and she didn't need me anymore," said Andrew, explaining his early return.

"We're all so glad," they said.

Dinner that night tasted especially good, and Andrew told everyone how he had missed them. When they questioned him about Auntie Lizard and what he had done there, Andrew simply answered, "I minded the shop."

Andrew's unasked questions were answered when they told him about Pooter's disappearance, and how worried they all had been.

After dinner Pooter followed Andrew to the tree house. Andrew looked at Pooter. "Did you set off to join me? It's just as well you didn't reach me. I could tell you things you wouldn't believe."

"I'd believe anything," said Pooter.

Andrew turned. "Pooter, did you say something?"

High in the treetop Andrew felt close to the sky. He wondered if the stars could be reached with magical powers. The more he looked at them the closer they got. And he could almost touch them.